Inked Hearts

LINDSAY DETWILER

HOT TREE
PUBLISHING

Inked Hearts © 2017 by Lindsay Detwiler

For information, contact the publisher, Hot Tree Publishing.

WWW.HOTTREEPUBLISHING.COM

EDITING: HOT TREE EDITING

COVER DESIGNER: CLAIRE SMITH

FORMATTER: RMGRAPHX

ISBN-10: 1-925655-08-3

ISBN-13: 978-1-925655-08-7

10 9 8 7 6 5 4 3 2 1

More From Lindsay

To all of the women

looking for themselves

Chapter One

Six years, a complex about my freckles, a love for pastrami, and a fear of failure.

That's what he gave me before slaughtering my heart and my faith in men.

To be fair, I'm a bit jaded now, my objectivity overpowered by the vision of him between the sheets with his secretary, Nora. Her perfectly tan body, the blonde hair, him moving on top of her, the look on their faces when I came home early....

"Focus," I shout like a crazy person. My mastiff Henry rustles in the back seat, stretched over duffle bags, a few beach towels, and some random household items. I flick on my left turn signal, peering over my shoulder to try to get a clear view of the lane beside me. It's next to impossible, since my tiny Suzuki's bogged down by the material contents of my life, or at least those things I deemed worthy enough to carry to the next phase. Always a precarious driver at best, I tell myself to breathe, say a little prayer, and swerve into the lane beside me. Mercifully, it works. We don't die.

I adjust my sunglasses on my head, a few flyaway strands of hair sticking to my hot-pink lip gloss and making me wish I opted for plain lips. But a girl changing her life… well, it felt like a pink lip gloss kind of day this morning.

I drive on, Keith Urban's songs and Henry's snoring my only company besides my warped memories and anxiety-ridden thoughts. The sun beats down, a few clouds wispy in the bright sky. It's a gorgeous day, a day screaming of redemption, of resurrection.

With nothing but time to think for the last two hours of my drive, my mind wanders to another dark place—the place beyond the bedroom escapades of my ex-husband. It travels to the place of doubt, the place so many family members and friends have played on in the past few weeks.

"You can start over without moving away," or, "Are you sure you need to move that far?" or, "Maybe you should just go for a month or something," seemed to be regular statements. Everyone thinks it's ludicrous. Women like me don't do this. Respectable women, introverted women, responsible women. They don't do this, not even if their husbands cheat on them.

Sure, they're on my side. My dad threatened to get out his shotgun and make the bastard pay. My mother droned on and on about how she always knew he was like this—no matter she'd said he was a real keeper on the day of our wedding. Friends, cousins, aunts, uncles, neighbors, even my garbageman all seemed anxious to jump on the "fuck, you, Chris," train. They were willing to throw around all types of murderous plots, and I got to see a side of them I didn't quite know existed.

But then, the weeks slipped by, and the rage, shock, and hurt of Chris cheating with his secretary faded for everyone else. Then they moved on to urging me to get out of my funk, to forget about him, to move on. I'm only twenty-eight, after all. I'm, in their words, young, vibrant, ready to find love again. Hell, most women don't even get married until almost thirty these days, they remind me—as if that's supposed to make me feel better. I could just forget about what happened, pretend he didn't exist, pretend the marriage didn't exist. I should stop wallowing in pity and get back to "normal" life, carrying on with my existence here. They think I can just blot him out of my life and continue on like nothing has changed. That I can just substitute in a new man and carry on as "Accountant" Avery as if everything is just peachy.

Easy for them to say.

How do you just forget about six years of your life? How do you pretend you aren't changed, broken by what happened? How do you just slap your heart back together, jolt it, and tell it to forget love hurts? How do you forget about the singed feeling of betrayal, the feeling of not being good enough, the feeling of being deceived? How do you rediscover your belief that love can last forever, when a single moment torched the ideal into dirty ashes? How do you not look at the restaurants and local haunts with a wistful eye, remembering the moments that had built up to a relationship that would only end in scorched hearts?

In hindsight, there are always warning signs. I'm sure there were at least a few I missed.

But to hell if I could see them. To hell if I can see them now. Thinking about it, I didn't see any forlorn looks between Chris and Nora. I didn't see any distant nights or turned-down passionate evenings. I didn't see a cold distance growing between us.

I saw love. Right up until the day I walked in and saw my whole life drown in screams and tears, I was happy with him. I'd thought he'd been happy with me.

No, it's not like I can look back and say, "Thank God it's over. I was tired of it all anyway." It's not like our marriage was marked by screaming fights on weeknights and sexless, passionless existences. Our marriage, in retrospect, seemed the thing of fairy tales. Despite the subtle clues I'm sure existed, it all seemed perfect. I felt like our vows were true, like we would remain faithful until death ripped us apart. I thought my marriage would stand the test of time up until the fateful moment when everything fell apart with a single early return home, a single moment, and more than a few "mistakes" on his part.

As clichéd as it sounds, it felt like the affair fell right out of the sky.

Now, six years of marriage has disintegrated down to a Suzuki full of random boxes, a complex for my freckles because he'd always told me it was a sign of sun damage, a love for his favorite food, pastrami, and a broken heart that will never truly be repaired.

Inhaling, I remind myself to also breathe. Lately, it

seems I have to remind myself to do that quite frequently.

Looking in the rearview mirror, I see the road behind me. The road is paved with love, loss, and quite a few regrets.

It's done now, though. Chris moved on, and so will I.

Not in the way everyone thinks I should, though. I won't return to my routine, piece back a semblance of the life I had with him. It's taken me almost a year, but I've realized I want something different.

Everyone's right. I'm young, although the deepening crow's feet don't always make me feel that way. I'm free now, too. I should live it up, be the wild twentysomething I never let myself be as an accountant and as his wife. I'll let go of the laundry schedule and the dinner by six o'clock ideal. I'll shake myself out of the pencil skirts and kitten-heeled shoes. I'll let go of the librarian bun Chris thought was sexy, and the perfect pearl earrings. I'm ready to let that woman go and find a new me, the me I never got a chance to explore.

I take another breath, almost smelling the salty sea, telling myself I'm ready to make this change, even if it is a little bit crazy.

"One hundred miles, Henry," I say as I peer in the rearview mirror. The dog just keeps snoring, his tongue actually hanging out of his loose muzzle and flopping on the seat. I smile.

Just one hundred more miles until I am no longer Avery, Chris's wife. One hundred more miles until I am no longer the scorned wife, the poor Avery who never saw it coming. One hundred more miles until I am no longer the fifty-hour work weeks in the office, family dinner on Sunday, laundry on Friday night Avery.

One hundred more miles until I am the new Avery, the woman I've always wanted to be but was too afraid of. One hundred more miles until I'm a brand-new woman without a past to haunt her, without pitying stares and questioning looks. One hundred miles until I break out of the perfect square constructed for my life. One hundred miles until I start fresh with new people, with a new town, with a new life. Only Henry knows my past, and I don't think he's telling anyone anything.

And the first thing I vow to myself in this new version of life?

I won't let a man change that again. I won't let a man control me, own my heart. I'll live for myself this time, wild and free, a girl of the unpredictable wind.

Chapter Two

My car screeches to a halt in the single open parking space behind the building. I check my phone again, ensuring the GPS is correct.

Yep, this is it. Home sweet home.

I try not to be too judgy as I stare at the peeling, vomit-green siding and the crooked sign in front of the Oceanview Apartments.

It's a small building filled with several living units. The website described it as "seaside sophistication at an affordable price."

I'm seeing affordable, but not much sophistication, especially considering the pink flamingo on the front lawn. Still, my new roommate—whom I also found online—insists the place is charming and within walking distance of so many of Ocean City's great places. She said there are plenty of places to work nearby. Plus, it accepts pets of all sizes, which is a good thing since Henry is over two hundred pounds. Life changers can't be choosers, I suppose.

My online search for a roommate was one of the major reasons my parents weren't so happy with my midtwenties crisis decision. I have a feeling one look at the external aspects of the Oceanview Apartments and they definitely wouldn't be fans.

"What if she's a serial killer?" Mom had shrieked when I told her about Jodie.

"Mom, look at her. Does she look like the serial-killing type?" I'd asked, showing her the picture of the redhead with an adorable pixie cut and perfectly white teeth.

"Well, you don't even know that's what she'll look like."

"Mom, really. It's fine. I've scoped her out."

She'd huffed, then given me nine hundred more reasons why this was a terrible idea. The inner teenager in me just liked it more and more as she kept talking.

If I'm being honest now, the butterflies in my stomach support my mom's fears that this is a mistake. Moving a state away, packing up my life into my old car and starting over, seems ridiculous. Finding a roommate online, coming here with no job, with no real plan—what was I thinking? The plan I made two months ago suddenly doesn't seem like a plan at all.

I barely know anything about this Jodie other than she needs a new roommate, she's a writer, and she loves the color purple, since all of her e-mails were in purple fonts.

Not too much to base a trusting roommate relationship on, I know.

It's too late now. I've made up my mind. It's time to see it through, serial killer or not.

"You ready to see our new home, Henry?" He just keeps snoring.

I get out of the car, finding Henry's leash on the passenger side floor beside a crumpled-up empty bag from McDonald's. I open the back door, a few boxes precariously falling as I do. I leave them, figuring I'll get them later. Henry sluggishly makes his way out of the car, stretching his stiff joints like an old man, and I hook up his leash.

I push my sunglasses higher on my nose, breathing in the salty air. We're a few blocks back from oceanfront, but I can hear the waves above the honking sounds of the cars. The humid air assaults my face and the wind causes my hair to stick to my lip gloss again, but I can't feel anything but happiness. This might be crazy. This might be a terrible idea. This might be completely out of character for the logical, rational accountant who has sticky notes on every surface of her office to plan out the month.

But with the beach waves in the background and the sun beaming down on me, I only feel one thing.

Free.

Henry pants dramatically already. Never one for the heat, this might not be his first choice of locale to move to. Still, there's a decent square of yard with each property, something tough to come by in a city dominated by concrete and sand. Plus, Jodie has air conditioners, a true plus.

We make our way to apartment 104, the one Jodie lives in. Correction—the one I now live in.

Her old roommate apparently got married and moved away, leaving her in a bind. She was happy to find someone so quickly. I'll admit, living with a roommate seems odd at this stage in life. I have some money in savings but don't want to bite into it all at once, especially with my current career status unknown. Plus, I don't like the idea of living alone. I guess I've watched way too many *Dateline* specials. Of course, if I listen to Mom, I'll end up on a two-hour special anyway.

We saunter to the front door and ring the doorbell. I slide my sunglasses to the top of my head, realizing what a momentous few minutes this will be. *I'm actually doing it.* I'm actually changing my life. Here goes nothing.

The door flies open, as if on cue.

"*Hi,*" a voice squeals with such animation, I instantly feel like I'm royalty.

Jodie is just as cute as the picture, her red hair framing her petite features. Her smile, though, is bigger than life, and despite her tiny frame, she seems to own the space, to own life with her personality.

I don't even have time to respond. She's wrapping her arms around me, hugging it out. I return the hug, not really expecting this type of welcome.

"This must be Henry, huh? Hey, big guy." Jodie crouches down, rubbing Henry's muzzle. His tail wags methodically, and before I can stop him, he's putting his paw on her shoulder, knocking her to the ground, and planting a huge, sloppy kiss on her.

"Oh my God, Henry, stop. I'm so sorry, he's usually better behaved than this," I rush to say, feeling like my new roommate is already going to evict us.

She just giggles loudly. "I love him already," she says, petting his head as he slurps her cheek, causing her to giggle even louder. I quickly pull him back, letting her stand up and brush herself off.

I'm not really sure what to say, but Jodie doesn't wait for me to feel awkward. "Well, are you coming in? It's home now. Better get in here and make it yours."

I smile, following her inside, knowing I already like her warmth. No serial killer vibes happening yet, which is a good thing.

Check one off Mom's ridiculously long worry list.

I take in the interior. It's… artsy. Huge abstract paintings hang everywhere. There's a really neat log coffee table in the center of the living room area, papers spewing out of every inch of the surface. It's definitely warm and inviting, just like Jodie, but also a bit disheveled. This girl's not a clean freak, which is okay by me.

This looks like the space to let go of some of my type A tendencies. It'll be good for me, I think, although inside, I do wonder how long until it's appropriate for me to rearrange the furniture in the room, because the layout isn't really making sense.

Before I can think about it too much, though, Henry's yanking on the leash. I try to assess the situation, to gain control, but before I know it, the leash is out of my hands, and Henry is barking and running inside the apartment.

"Henry," I say again, terrified he's going to break something. Online, I'd told Jodie Henry was super well-behaved. Yeah, not really looking that way.

"Sebastian! Come here, baby. Stop teasing him."

I see a flash of fluffy gray running, Henry chasing after it, his tail and leash knocking down papers and knickknacks.

I try to stop him, chasing in a pointless, endless circle. It's hopeless, and I have visions of the entire apartment being destroyed.

The fluffy gray ball of fur named Sebastian finally perches on a shelf up high in the living room. Henry sits below him, barking. I shush him, and he mercifully obeys, but not before emitting a tiny-dog-style whine.

"I am so sorry again," I say, grabbing my head. "I didn't realize you had a cat. Henry's never been around them. I'm so sorry."

Jodie smiles warmly at me, waving a hand dismissively. "It's no big deal, it's fine."

I eye the papers, some of which are now shredded on the ground. "Oh my gosh, your papers. Let me get them," I say, reaching for them, not sure what to do. This is turning out to be a disaster. Almost worse than a serial killer situation.

"Don't be silly. They're just chapters for my book. No biggie."

A writer. She's a writer, she told me that. And now Henry's ruined her book? This just can't get worse.

"Oh God, your book? He's probably ruined them. I'm so sorry," I apologize again.

Jodie stops me. "Will you stop apologizing? It's fine, really. I have the important stuff transferred to my computer. And what I don't have transferred, well, apparently it wasn't good enough. The universe was just trying to tell me to do a better job." She skips to the kitchen, opening the fridge. I stand staring at the cat, at Henry, at the papers, in awe of her calm demeanor.

Maybe she *is* a serial killer.

Jodie returns with two wine coolers. It's barely past noon. Nevertheless, when she hands one to me, I claim it, needing something to calm my nerves.

She clears off a space on the couch. "So, roomie. What do you think of the place?" she asks before taking a swig of her drink.

"It's really nice. I love how close it is to the ocean. Thanks again for taking me on."

"Please. You're doing me a huge favor. It's been too quiet around here. I can't work in quiet. I need noise. I need life. This is going to be spectacular for my writing."

I turn to see Henry still staring at Sebastian. "I'm sorry. I don't know what to do with him. I don't want him bothering your cat."

"Oh, it's fine. Sebastian just showed up at my door a few days ago. It was raining, and he looked hungry. I took him to the vet yesterday, got him a bath. Figured he found me, so I was meant to help him, you know? I know I didn't tell you I had a cat when we talked, but I knew you were an animal lover and would be okay with it."

"Oh, yeah. It's fine. I'm just worried about them getting along."

Jodie waves a hand. "You worry a lot, huh?"

It's a strangely deep question, not quite the small talk I'm ready for. "Maybe," I say.

"Well, stop. No more worrying. Beach life is different. You've got to go with the flow, right, Avery?"

"Yeah. I'm going to try."

"Good. Well, listen, why don't you go ahead and get yourself settled. Your room is the last on the right down the hallway. Don't tiptoe around. It's home now. Treat it that way."

"Great. Thank you."

"No thank-yous. It's home, remember? You're not a guest."

"Okay. Got it."

I stand awkwardly, still not feeling like it's home. I head to my car to get a few boxes. Jodie stands. "Need some help?"

"Sure, if you don't mind."

"Not a problem." We head to my Suzuki, and she says, "Cute car. Love it."

"Thanks. It's okay. I've had it since college. Can't stand to part with it." I hand her one of the boxes. She peeks inside the car.

"Is this everything?" She motions toward the boxes in my car.

I shrug. "Everything I felt was important enough."

"Interesting."

"What's interesting?"

"Just interesting to think about having to find the important stuff. Must mean you had a lot of clutter in your life, that's all."

"Are you always so deep?"

"Avery, honey, I told you. I'm a writer. We read way too much into everything."

I grin. "I see that. But in this case, you're right. I had a lot of clutter. I'm trying to get rid of it, though, start over."

"A man, right?"

"What?"

"It was a man?"

"Yeah. An ex-husband."

"I figured when you e-mailed me. I could tell by the way you said 'starting fresh.' Anyway, this is a good place to do it. Give it a few months. You'll be having so much fun, you won't even know his name. I'll make sure of it. I'm going to show you what the twenties are really about, Avery."

"I'm sure you will. But in the meantime, do you know of anyone who's hiring? I don't have a job lined up."

"No job? Talk about starting fresh."

"Hey, you said go with the flow."

"Yeah, but I also said make sure you can pay your rent," she says, but there isn't a serious note in her voice. She smiles, carrying a box as I follow.

"Well, then you better help me find somewhere good."

"Oh, I have somewhere good. I've even got an in. I'll take you there tomorrow."

"Great. Thank you."

Jodie turns to me. I smile. "Sorry. I forgot. Cancel the thank-you."

"You ungrateful bitch," she says, and my eyes widen, but she just laughs again. I shake my head. This girl is crazy. Warm, exuberant… but crazy.

She's just the kind of roommate I need.

"So anyway, I never got to ask you what kind of novels you write," I say as we return to the living room, Henry still staring at a hissing Sebastian.

"Horror," she says, and I shake my head.

Maybe the serial killer worry isn't off the table yet.

Chapter Three

I awake to the sound of scratching, something I'm not used to. Sun shining way too brightly in my face—I really need to get some room darkening blinds for in here—I roll onto my side, groggily trying to assess the source of the sound. Henry, lying beside me with his head on one of my pillows, doesn't even blink, snoring right through the noise.

Some guard dog.

It takes me a moment to orient myself, the bright purple walls foreign compared to the pale green walls in my bedroom at home.

Correction. This is now home. Bright purple it is.

I sit up, rubbing sleep out of my eyes while probably smearing mascara. I shake out my hair, stretch, and decide to get some coffee.

The scratching continues. Apparently Sebastian wants to be friends with Henry. Or get him evicted.

I prepare to saunter into the kitchen, but reassess my idea. Looking down, I realize I'm braless and wearing my worn-out sweatpants from college—the ones with a hole in the thigh and are almost threadbare. This whole roommate thing is out of my league. Do I need to get dressed first? Do my hair? Brush my teeth? The thought of walking out there in front of anyone, let alone a near stranger, seems inappropriate. The thought of putting real pants on at this hour, though, seems out of the question.

Figuring I might as well take Jodie's advice and make myself at home, I opt for a thin sweatshirt to throw over my faded T-shirt before slinking out to find coffee.

Which reminds me—I don't have any coffee. I really need to get to the store. This whole "go with the flow" lifestyle isn't all it's cracked up to be, I suppose.

I chastise myself for being so negative, for resorting to the old Avery ways of being the rational planner. I can make this work. I need to give it a go.

I open the door, and Sebastian dashes into my room, no doubt to stir Henry. I decide to trust Jodie. I worry too much. They'll work it out.

I head out to the island in the kitchen.

"Hey, roomie. How'd you sleep? Sorry, I really like the word 'roommate'. I'm actually writing a story right now about roommates, so I guess that's why I'm using it too much."

I manage a grin, although I'm barely following Jodie's mile-a-minute speech. She's on the sofa, typing away on her laptop while she turns to talk at me. She's chipper, completely awake. It looks like she's been up for hours.

Pretty sure I don't look like I'm even conscious right now.

I do feel better that she's at least in yoga pants and a T-shirt. My attire is apparently okay.

"I slept fine," I say.

"You don't look like it," she says, then flashes me a huge smile. I'm already learning Jodie is one of those people who are just so darn likable, they can say anything. She can basically tell me I look like shit and then smile, and it somehow doesn't seem offensive.

I like that, though.

"Okay, truth. It's just not quite feeling like home yet."

"Well, that's because we need to add your flavor to the place, make it you. Especially in your room. Maybe after work today, we can swing by the home décor shop, pick up some things." She puts her laptop on the coffee table, and heads to the kitchen. "Coffee, yes? It's in the top cupboard over there. Hope you like bold roast."

"I like any roast right now. I'll restock your supplies later. I need to go to the store."

Jodie waves a hand. "It's fine. Please. It's a cup of coffee, Avery, not a car. Give yourself some time to get settled."

Before I can even get to the cupboard, she skips over to the coffee maker, popping a pod in the Keurig and sticking a mug that says Believe underneath it. Even her mugs scream chipper.

"So did I hear you right?" I ask as I plop myself onto one of the wooden stools by the island. "Did you say work?"

"Yeah, you did say you needed a job, right? I called Lysander yesterday. He said you've got the job."

I raise an eyebrow. "Who's Lysander? And what job?"

She shakes her head. "I'm sorry. I tend to get ahead of myself. Lysander owns Midsummer Nights. I know, crazy original, right?"

I just stare, not quite getting the reference.

Jodie smiles. "Not a Shakespeare fan?"

"No, not particularly. Math was my thing."

"Oh, right, the whole accountant thing. Well, Lysander's mom was an English teacher and she was a Shakespeare fan, hence Lysander's name. She owned the restaurant up until she died a few years ago. She named the restaurant Midsummer Nights because, well, it was her favorite play. The customers don't even believe us when we tell them the owner's name is actually Lysander."

I just nod.

"You still don't get it, huh? Well, one of these days, you'll have to read it. Anyway, there I go, getting ahead of myself," she says, shaking her head before grabbing my coffee for me. "Cream?"

"No, black coffee is fine."

Jodie gasps. I turn to see what's wrong. Seeing nothing, I turn back to her. This girl's giving me whiplash.

"What is it?" I finally ask, still confused about Shakespeare and jobs and now her fear.

"Nothing, it's just I read this study the other day how people who drink black coffee are more likely to be serial killers. And, well, this is sort of embarrassing, but when I told my mom about finding you online, she was terrified you were a serial killer."

I stare for a moment in silence, taking in everything.

Then, I burst out laughing.

"My mom thought the same thing."

Jodie grins. "It's sort of like fate, huh?"

"I suppose."

"Anyway," she says, now sitting at a stool herself as I warm my hands on the cup of coffee. "I waitress at Midsummer several days a week to help supplement my income. I talked to Lysander about you, and he actually could use another waitress. I mean, the money's not great, but the tips on weekends are killer. Midsummer's actually a pretty popular spot. And it would at least be a start, you know, until you figure out what you want to do."

A waitress. Not exactly what I had in mind, especially considering I've got a four-year degree plus a CPA certification. Still, it's a start. A fresh start. A chance to give up some of the restrictions of the business world, take some time to figure out what I want to be.

"Waitressing sounds great. But don't I need an interview or something?"

Jodie waves her hand. "It's fine, it's fine. Lysander trusts me. We know each other well."

"But you barely know me," I offer.

"True. But I'm a good judge of character. The first moment I saw you standing at my door, I knew you were okay, Avery. You've got an aura of kindness."

"An aura of kindness?" I raise an eyebrow, skeptical yet also flattered.

"I don't know how else to explain it. Anyway, drink your coffee, get yourself awake, and then we'll get going later this afternoon. We need to get there early so I can show you around. Midsummer has its quirks. I want to make sure you get off on the right foot."

"Thanks," I say.

"Remember what I said about not saying thanks?"

"I know. But I appreciate it."

"I know you do. Now listen, I'm going to go write for a little while. Take your time, explore the neighborhood, and then we'll head into work this afternoon."

"Okay. Sounds good. I'm just going to take Henry out to pee."

"I should probably feed Sebastian. Have you seen him?"

I realize I haven't seen him since he wandered into my room, and I haven't heard from Henry.

I scamper to my feet, tiptoeing to my room to peek in. Henry still sleeps on my bed, his kicking feet telling me he's in the middle of an intense dream.

There's an addition, though. Curled up right next to him is Sebastian. It sounds like he might be snoring a little, too.

I motion for Jodie, and she tiptoes over to my door. I point, and she smiles. "See, told you that you worry too much. Fast friends."

"Fast friends," I say, exhaling a breath I hadn't realized I'd been holding.

Chapter Four

"Hey, it's going to be fine," Jodie assures me, patting me on the back. I'm slumped over the counter in the kitchen, sweat trickling down my face. I've been running all afternoon and evening, and I'm exhausted. This desk-job girl isn't used to a physical job like this. Plus, it doesn't help that tonight's basically been a disaster.

Lysander comes flying through the back, exhaling audibly. This is it, I realize. He's coming back to say I'm done. My steps toward a new life are failing miserably, and I'm about to get fired for the first time in my life. Time to face the music.

"I'm so sorry, really. I know I'm a disaster—"

Lysander tosses his hand up in a motion that looks like something the Dog Whisperer uses to shush a barking dog. I, under normal circumstances, may have been offended. However, considering I'm basically destroying the man's business, I guess I could let it slide.

"Listen. It's fine. So you spilled a few drinks on a few customers. It'll be okay. I gave them some drinks on the house, and they don't even care anymore."

"In fairness, it was more than a few. I think I'm up to like five," I say, grimacing.

"Like I said, not a big deal."

"But what about the mixed-up orders? Plus, Georgette is pissed at me because I keep misunderstanding her."

Lysander shrugs, looking over his shoulder at Georgette, who is dancing by the grill as she whips up some burgers. He leans in. "Listen, I rarely understand what she says. She mumbles. Usually, I just grin and nod. So no big deal. Georgette's forgiving and forgetful. She'll be none the wiser by tomorrow."

I look over at the pleasantly plump older lady. She doesn't really seem like the grudge-holding type, I suppose.

"And then I can't remember a freaking thing. Like, I keep forgetting what key to push on the register. I keep forgetting what menu items are. I still have no idea what a Love-in-Idleness is."

"Oh, that's the flower in the play that makes the love potion." Jodie interrupts as she shoves a cheese fry in her mouth. She's on break, too—Joseph and Addie, who are also employees, are manning the tables right now.

"Okay, great. But what the heck is it on the menu?"

"It's my specialty," Lysander says, heading out of the kitchen. He is apparently owner and bartender here, according to Jodie. "Be right back," he calls over his shoulder.

I'm still not convinced things are okay, and I'm not sure why Lysander is being so nice to me.

"Isn't he the best?" Jodie says, offering me a cheese fry.

"He is. Which is why I feel even worse."

"Will you stop. Are you trying to get fired? Seriously. Let it go. You're too uptight. Loosen up. Stop worrying."

Jodie passes me a cheese fry, and I oblige, realizing I'm starving from all the stress and running. A few moments later, Lysander shoves through the swinging doors to the kitchen.

"Here," Lysander says, handing me a tall class of blue liquid.

"What's in it?"

"Magic," Lysander says, grinning.

I shrug, thinking about what Jodie's said. It's true. I came here to let go, to live a little. So what if I suck at my job? I shrug, take a tentative sip of the blue liquid. It's pretty good. Okay, it's really good, like a tart, fruity concoction that can only be described as magical. If I had to describe it, though, I would say it kind of reminds me of a Long Island mixed with blueberries and Swedish Fish. I decide to drink more, but Lysander pulls the cup away.

"I think that's enough for your first taste of Love-in-Idleness. You can finish it after your shift. I think you've spilled enough drinks sober."

I nod in agreement. "I should get back out there. As long as you still want me working."

"Look, I'm not firing you. Jodie assures me you're a math whiz and a great person. So you've got a job here as long as you want."

"Jodie barely knows me," I offer.

"Are you always so pragmatic?" Lysander asks. "Listen, she's a great judge of character."

"Damn straight. You better say that or I'll tell Reed about it."

"Who's Reed?"

"You'll meet him later," Jodie says, winking. "Now get your butt back out there and practice waitressing."

I smile, Lysander and Jodie both giving me a thumbs-up.

I don't know why the hell they believe in me or why they want to keep me around. As I head back to the tables, though, and take a deep breath, I realize how good it feels to already have a support system, a group of friends, and a place where I belong.

***

I spend the next two hours perfecting my waitressing game. Okay, so not quite perfecting. Just surviving, in all reality.

I manage to only spill one more drink—a Love-in-Idleness—and mess up one more order. I win Georgette over by complimenting her pies in the front display case. I actually make a few tips, and I don't piss any more customers off by making them wait too long for their checks.

But I'm so busy, I don't have time to stop and think about how crazy it all is. I don't have time to think about how this isn't how I ever expected my life to go. I don't have time to think about how this might not work out.

Most of all, I don't have time to think about him. I don't think about his favorite food or think about how he would kiss me on a summer night like tonight. I don't think about all our memories like a sappy montage from a romantic movie. For the first time in months, I don't spend the evening hours moping around, thinking about Chris and what could've been.

Or what should've been.

Which is a beautiful thing.

When Lysander turns the sign on the Shakespearean statue out front to "closed" and the final rowdy group of twentysomethings leaves, I lean on the counter by the register. I've never been this tired in my life. Computers and spreadsheets don't even come close to exhausting me the way this job has.

"So, you survived your first night," Lysander says, bringing me over another drink. I oblige, taking a sip. "What do you think of the place?"

I take a moment to look around, really looking at Midsummer Nights like I haven't had a chance to do. It's an odd mix of Victorian-England-style décor and a beachy vibe. There are abstract prints of the Bard himself all around. In some, he's surfing or wearing floral print shirts. Behind the bar, a quote is scrawled on the rustic paneling: "Lord, what fools these mortals be!" I'm assuming it's from the play. Maybe sometime I'll actually give it a read.

Despite the name and décor, there's not much Shakespearean about the food other than Lysander's specialty. It's your typical beachy pub food, which is fine by me. I'll just have to be careful too many cheese fries don't sneak up on my waistline.

Looking at Lysander, who is still awaiting my answer, I smile. "I think it's just what I need."

He beams with pride, a pride I know he takes in this place. "In some odd way, I think this place needs you too," he replies.

"Why? Do you need to get rid of a few customers or something?"

"It does get pretty packed in here on the weekends," Jodie chimes in, tossing me a rag to start cleaning the counter. "Enough sentimental crap. Get cleaning. I want to get home."

I grin at Jodie's bluntness and start wiping the table. As we're cleaning up, a tall blond saunters right past the "closed" sign, tossing the door open and strolling in. He heads straight for Lysander, whose face lights up.

"Hey, baby," Lysander says, and the two embrace. I look away, not wanting to creep on them.

"You better get used to it. Those two are crazy about each other," Jodie says. "Get a room already, will you?" she shouts as the two kiss.

They pull away, obliging Jodie.

"Honestly. If I'd have known I had to see you two so sickeningly in love every day, I would've never matched you up. You know, not all of us are having such a great time with love. It would be nice if you didn't rub it in our faces every single day." She grimaces, but I can tell she's not actually mad.

The blond walks toward me. "Who's this?"

"Reed, meet Avery Johannas. She's our new waitress.

Avery, this is Reed, my boyfriend," Lysander says. I put down the cleaning rag to reach for Reed's hand. He grasps it firmly, giving me a huge grin.

"Nice to meet you," I say.

"You won't be saying that in a few. This one never goes away," Jodie teases. Reed shakes his head.

"You're the one who kept me around."

"Don't remind me."

"So you introduced them?" I ask, wanting to be filled in.

"Yeah. This one," she says, pointing to Reed, "kept coming in here almost every night. He moved here from Philadelphia, and said we had the best cheesesteaks in town. I knew he had his eye on more than cheesesteaks, though. But Lysander thought I was crazy, convinced Reed had his eye on me. I finally broke the ice, asked Reed if he was gay, and the rest is history. You'd think a gay man would have better gaydar than a straight woman, but I guess not." She turns to Lysander, who is putting away some liquor and rolling his eyes. "Men. Straight or gay, they're all idiots," she adds, heading back to the kitchen to tidy up.

"Don't listen to her. She's just mad because she had her eye on me," Reed says, winking.

"I heard that, you liar," Jodie shouts from the back of the kitchen.

I can't help but laugh.

"So, Avery, what brings you to Ocean City?"

I shrug, wondering how much to confess. I don't really want to turn this into a serious counseling session like it could if I tell him the truth. I don't really want to admit how desperate I am to forget, how I'm a scorned woman needing a change. I don't want to see the pity in their eyes I've seen so many times before. So, instead of telling them the whole sordid story of Chris, I say, "Just needed a change, a new start. I was an accountant at my dad's CPA firm back home. I woke up and realized it wasn't what I wanted anymore."

It's partially true. Even without the whole situation with Chris, I was getting sort of bored with my job. As kind as Lysander has been, as much as I like him and Reed already, I'm not quite ready to lay out the whole "I got cheated on" story. Not yet.

"I get that," Reed says. "I was an actuary back in Philadelphia. I came here for a new start, too. Plus, I guess you could say there were some things going on with family."

"Where do you work now?" I ask.

"Well, I actually have a gift shop on the boardwalk. It's called Sand Dollars. Stop by sometime."

I smile. "I will."

"Okay, let's get out of here for the night, huh?" Lysander says. "We'll clean the rest tomorrow. I'm beat."

"Not too beat, I hope," Reed says, winking.

"And there's our cue," Jodie says, flying back out to the main area. "Let's get out of here, Avery. Leave these two lovebirds to their own devices before I gag."

"Don't worry, Jo. I'm still keeping my eye open for your next hunk," Reed says.

"Too bad all the good ones are taken. Or gay."

"I know I set the bar high. But we'll find you a hetero hunk. I promise."

"I won't get my hopes up," she says, and I follow her out the door. Once we're outside, she tells me, "Last guy those two found for me turned out to be an ex-convict. Not sure I'm trusting their judgement."

I smile. "They seem nice," I say as we head to Jodie's car.

"They are. Honestly. Even if my writing made enough money to support me, I'd still probably keep working there. It's not really a job, you know? Lysander makes it more like family."

"I see that. I like it. Thank you."

Jodie gives me the death glare. "No need to thank me, remember?"

"I remember. But still, I appreciate it."

"I know. And once you settle in, you'll like it even more. Those two are great, the tips are good, and there is never a shortage of hot guys coming in."

"Well, they're all yours, Jodie. I'm done with men right now."

"Well, there are hot women, too."

"No, I don't mean it like that. I'm straight. I just…. It's been a rough year. I'm just not ready for love. I don't think I'll ever be."

"How about a one-night stand? Are those off the table, too?"

"For now."

"No fun," Jodie says, scowling. "He must've done a number on you."

"He did," I say, looking out the window at the streetlights

and crowds of partying vacationers meandering on the side streets. For a moment, the melancholy comes creeping back, the sense of loss, the sense of fear.

"Well, screw him," Jodie says. "You're going to be better off."

I turn to look at my new, crazy redheaded friend and roommate. "I hope you're right," I say into the darkness, offering up a wish and a prayer to the stars that she's right.

Chapter Five

"Hey, Mom, sorry. I was sleeping. I worked the late shift last night. How are you?"

It's been a week since my move, and I've already settled into a routine, despite my best efforts to stay spontaneous. Between my shifts at Midsummer Nights and my attempt to get settled, I really don't have the free time I thought I would. It's all good though.

Midsummer has turned out to be a blessing, my job so different from my stuffy office back in Pennsylvania. Most of all, it's a new start. There are no memories of us here. I don't have to walk past our old haunts, see our old friends, or be transported to our old moments. Chris isn't anywhere here. It's completely devoid of him, even if my heart isn't quite yet. I'm definitely making progress.

"Hey, honey. How are you doing? Ready to come home yet?" Mom never toys around, always jumping right to the punchline.

"Mom, we've been over this."

"I know. But I think you're making a mistake."

I sigh audibly, flopping backward on my bed, staring at the ceiling as I twirl a piece of hair. We've had this conversation at least thirty times.

"You've said that already. But I'm here now. I'm happy. This is what I need."

There's an awkward pause before she speaks again. I don't even really have to listen to what she says. I know what's coming. "You know, Dad is having a really hard time finding someone to fill your shoes. I've barely seen him all week because he's having to help pick up some of the responsibilities."

Bingo. If appealing to my rational sense doesn't work, Mom dives right into the guilt trip.

"He had plenty of notice to get someone. He's just being picky."

"I just don't understand why you'd want to give up your career. I know Chris hurt you, but that's no reason to throw your life away."

Anger builds now. "It's not throwing my life away, Mom. That life wasn't making me happy."

"And working a menial job, living with some girl you don't even know in an unfamiliar town is going to make you happy?"

"I don't know," I admit. "But it's worth a try."

Sensing there's nothing else to say, Mom shifts the conversation to other topics. She mentions my brother Blane and how he's doing so well in med school.

Of course he is. He's a damn genius.

She talks about her new nail technician, about the sale at Macy's, and about how Fluffers the cat needs to go to the groomers again. She goes on and on about things that used to matter to me.

But something has shifted. I've shifted. Suddenly, the talk about manicure appointments and designer shoes doesn't really seem so meaningful. It seems like a reminder I've done the right thing. I've escaped a life certainly teeming with more luxuries... but certainly emptier, too.

I hang up with Mom, promising to come and visit in the next month or so.

I love my parents and am grateful for all the opportunities they gave me, don't get me wrong.

Nonetheless, being here away from the pressures of family and work, I'm starting to see how good it feels to be out from under their watchful eye. I'm starting to see what it's like to be just Avery, not Avery the accountant, Avery the wife, Avery the daughter of the CPA firm's owner. I'm seeing what it's like to take charge, to make choices, to live.

I don't know if this is the answer to my life, or if Midsummer Nights is actually a wise career move. The thing is, though, staring at this ceiling in this tiny room, I don't care if it's wise. For once in my life, I don't care about doing the smart thing, the rational thing, or the acceptable thing.

I care about doing the thing that makes me happy.

As Henry leaps onto the bed with me, I realize that for the first time in a long time, I inexplicably am.

***

Jodie tosses a skimpy tank top at me.

"What's this?" I say, holding up a shirt I wouldn't have been caught dead in a few weeks ago. The flashy yellow color only adds to my initial dislike.

"Your outfit. Let's go. We're going out."

It's Friday night, and we're both off from Midsummer Nights. Lysander's actually shut the place down, vowing the loss of profits will be worth it for a night out, a night away from the stress of the business. I have big plans—sleeping, Netflix, and maybe a pint of Ben & Jerry's to celebrate.

"Come on. You're already falling into a rut. You came here for a change. Mix it up, already," she orders before stomping out of the room to go finish her makeup. She's already wearing a denim mini and a black halter.

I sigh, not really wanting to change out of my leggings, let alone put this shirt—and I use the word "shirt" loosely—on. Still, Jodie's right. I'm already falling into a rut. I need to step out of my comfort zone, explore a little. I came here for a new way of living, not to fall into a slumpy divorcee routine.

I slink into the top, finagling the straps so all my cleavage doesn't completely topple out—not like there's much there to topple out, anyway. I squeeze into some jeans and my favorite ballet flats. Glancing in the mirror at my hair, I decide it isn't too bad. I turn to look at my back, and my fingers graze the heart on my left shoulder. Ugh. I hate the prospect of it sticking out, the date in the center a slap in the face. There's nothing I can do about it, though, other than try to forget it.

A little fluffing and some spritzing of my hair, and I'm actually feeling okay, tattoo aside. Maybe I should let my hair grow a little to cover it. That's a worry for another day, though.

I hear a catcall from the hallway and turn to see Jodie appraising me. "Hot mama, not bad," she says. I roll my eyes. "You're going to have to shove the men off you."

"I'm not—"

"Looking for a man, I know," she interrupts. "Too bad. Here, put on some lips and let's go." She tosses me a tube of bright red lipstick, a shade I haven't worn in a long time. Chris hated red lips. I shove the thought aside as I slather on a coating.

"Wow, look at that. I didn't know you were inked," Jodie says, admiring my shoulder. I pull back self-consciously.

"Chris and I got them when we got married."

"Yuck, we need to take care of that," Jodie says, not even trying to cover her thoughts. I smile at her frankness, shaking my head.

"Be good, Henry," I say a few minutes later as we head out the door. I head for my car, but Jodie just leads me toward the street.

"We can walk. We're not going far. There's an awesome club a few blocks down called the Marooned Pirate. It's a good place for twentysomethings like us."

"The Marooned Pirate? Sounds terrible."

"Come on, grandma. Loosen up. Stick with me, and I'll show you how to live like a real twentysomething. You've been living the boring married life too long."

I can't really argue. She's right. Still, I feel anxiety rise in my chest. This is *so* not my scene. My scene for the past few years has been mismatched flannel pajamas on the sofa reading *Glamour* while Chris worked on his computer. My scene has been some *CSI* on a really "rowdy" night with a Coca-Cola if I was feeling risqué. My scene was folding laundry on a Friday night and tucking in early to get some extra sleep.

Now, though, I'm prancing down the dark street with a wild, free-spirited writer. I'm wearing a yellow top that looks more like a bra and potentially covers even less. I've got what Chris would call "hooker lipstick" on, and I'm about to head to a club for the first time in I don't even know how long.

It's exactly what I should be doing, I remind myself. However, you can take the woman out of the marriage, but you can't take the married mindset out of the woman. I feel dirty and awkward.

When we get to the Marooned Pirate, though, the exuberance of the atmosphere, the loud music, and the laughing twentysomethings free me. I take in the scene like a child at the mall near Christmastime, the flashy lights and sounds calling out to me. I revel in the energy, and before I know it, I, too, feel pretty energetic.

"Isn't it great?" Jodie yells over the music before leading me to the bar for some shots.

I don't try to rationalize why I shouldn't do this, or try to be responsible. Instead, I take the glass from Jodie's hand when she offers it to me. "To a fresh start," I say in a mock toast.

"To loosening up," Jodie says, winking as she holds her shot up, too. I toss back the fiery liquid, jump up and down a little, and smile at what I hope is the start of a new, freer life.

A few hours in, and I'm dancing like no one is watching—although quite a few people are probably staring at my questionable dance moves. Lysander and Reed eventually show up and buy me another round of drinks. We dance the night away, the four of us laughing and having a blast. A few guys ask me if I'm single. I just say "No," even my inebriated state not breaking down the barrier in my heart. A few guys ask Jodie if she's single, and she says, "Hell yes." Her single heart isn't bound by the chains of the past like a heart that's been through divorce. I'm sure Jodie's had her demons. Still, I envy her a little—her wily heart, her all-in emotions.

As Jodie dances with a hunky, tanned muscle-man, I sit at the bar with Reed and Lysander.

"So what did he do to you?" Reed asks, leaning in. I find it hard to focus on his face, too many shots mixing with the margarita for a toxic concoction in my bloodstream. "Who?"

"Your ex. Your face is painted with the despair of a broken heart, a broken marriage."

"You got me. He cheated on me. I walked in on the whole scene." I don't hold back this time, the alcohol loosening my lips like it always does.

"Ouch, honey." Reed puts an arm around me, and Lysander flags down a bartender for another drink.

"Yeah, it sucks. It was his secretary. A sexy little blonde."
Maybe it's the booze or maybe it's just the realization that no
matter how hard I try, I'll never be quite free of what Chris
did to me. Regardless, the bright yellow top is suddenly
looking garish, and the club is way too loud. The music,
the drinks—it can't change the facts. Chris didn't want me
anymore. I wasn't good enough. I didn't make him happy.
Why wasn't I good enough? Tears well up.

"Oh no you don't," Lysander says, sticking another
margarita in my hand.

"I can't drink this," I say, pushing it toward him.

"Yes, you can. There's only one answer to a fucked-up
heart and a cheating husband. Alcohol."

I know I've had way more than I should. I'm a lightweight
to begin with. I haven't had this much to drink since college.
Still, the frosty glass feels good in my hand. The thought of
drinking my heart into oblivion sounds good, too. So, I hold
the glass to my lips and take another sip.

"I love you, guys," I say to Lysander and Reed.

"Everyone does, darling," Reed retorts, nudging me
with his shoulder. "Now enough pitying yourself. Let's get
out there and dance, girl."

And we do. We dance like I'm not carrying a shattered
heart in my chest, like I'm just some twentysomething
living for the present.

***

"I'm never listening to you again," I murmur, stumbling
to the kitchen, my eyes bleary and head pounding.

Jodie, whose hair is all over the place and mascara is streaking her cheeks, is already sitting at the island, downing a cup of coffee. She looks rough, but not as rough as I feel.

"Here, sunshine. Take these and you'll feel better." She hands me two ibuprofen. I don't even hesitate, shoving them into my mouth immediately.

"I feel terrible."

"But you had fun last night, didn't you?" she asks, grinning as she types away on her laptop. Henry plods up to me, letting out a groan. The prospect of taking him out into the sunshine suddenly seems intolerable. I feel like a vampire.

"I'll get him," Jodie says, and I could kiss her feet.

"Why don't you look as bad as I feel?" I ask, slumping to the stool at the island.

"I'm conditioned for this. Don't worry, a few more weekends, and you'll be used to it."

"Is this really how people live?"

"You shouldn't have to ask that. But yes," she says as she leashes up Henry to take him outside.

Jodie is back with Henry before I've even been tempted to move. Even the prospect of pouring a coffee seems too laborious. How the hell did I let this happen? Never again, I swear.

"So, do you have any plans for today?" Jodie asks.

"Other than dying? No."

"Good. Because I made plans for us this afternoon."

"Aren't you going to let me recover? I know I said I wanted to live it up a bit, but can't we ease into it?"

"Relax. No alcohol or clubs. Something that needs to be done, though."

"What?" I ask.

Jodie touches her shoulder. I don't get it.

"Your tattoo," she says. "Your matchy-matchy tattoo with Chris. It's got to go. You're starting over. You don't need that reminder."

I grimace, fluffing my hair. I stand and head for the coffeepot. "Yeah, well, not much I can do about it."

"There's plenty we can do about it. I know this great tattoo shop. The owner is amazing. He does a ton of cover-ups and stuff. I once made a terrible mistake and got a matching tattoo with a boyfriend. The boyfriend ended up being a drug addict and we broke up. This guy was able to redesign it. See, look," she says, pulling up her shirt to show me a fancy tree on her ribs. The tree is adorned with scattered hearts.

"Cute," I say, meaning it.

"Yeah, well you know what wasn't so cute? The devil it used to be."

I smirk. She looks serious. "Wait, you mean a real devil? Like horns and all?"

"Yeah. Bright red, too. The guy had some interesting beliefs. I was young and in love. But Jesse covered it right up."

"How did you come across this guy?"

"He comes to Midsummer Nights most Tuesdays. I would've pointed him out, but we haven't both worked a Tuesday night together yet. Anyway, he's awesome. I called just now, and he has an opening. Let's get rid of that heart that makes me gag just looking at it."

"What would I get instead?"

"Anything you want. This is about you, Avery. So what do you say?"

I take a sip of my coffee, eyeing this zany girl who is definitely not letting me fall into a boring rut again. I absentmindedly touch the heart on my shoulder, thinking about what it means. For a moment, my mind flashes back to the night a week after our wedding. We were two twenty-one-year-olds high on life and the newlywed feeling. I remember squealing when we looked at them in the mirror, the matching tattoos a symbol of our matching forevers.

Now, though, the tattoo is just a reminder that we're broken, that I'm one piece leftover of the ill-fated duo. Now, when I see the tattoo, all I see is the look on his face when we said our goodbyes, when he chose Nora over me. All I see is a symbol of our brokenness, of my brokenness, of a destroyed love.

"Okay. I'll do it. But no devils."

"Deal. Sober up. We don't have to be there for a few hours."

"This guy's good, right?" I ask again, feeling a little nervous.

"Honey, don't worry. You'll be in good hands. Really nice, sexy, manly hands, in fact." Jodie gives me a wink. I shake my head, taking my coffee out to the living room to catch up on some news.

My mind wanders over the next few hours, thinking

about the prospect of a new start, even with my tattoos. This is really happening. The Avery I've always wanted to be is surfacing. I can't wait to see her in her full, shining glory.

***

I readjust my bra strap, a little self-conscious that I wore my supersexy, superlacy red one. I should've gone more conservative. At least it isn't the graying, grandma-like bra I sometimes toss on. I forgot the tattoo artist would be seeing a lot more of me than any man has in a while.

I shake off the jitters as Jodie leads me through the door of J & J's Tattoos. We're two blocks back from the famous Ocean City boardwalk, the corner lot almost overlookable in the busy streets. The front is a chic black, and I have to admit, the shop looks classy and clean, not like the stereotypical tattoo parlors people imagine.

Not that I actually know much about tattoo parlors, in all fairness. I've only been to one.

I take a deep breath and study the inside of J & J's. There's a little waiting area with black leather chairs. A large bald man sits in one—actually, more like two—seats. He's very sweaty and is tapping his foot anxiously. Pretty sure this is his first tattoo. He looks more than a bit nervous. I offer him a weak smile, but he just continues to look like he's going to faint or vomit any second.

Next to him is a group of giggling girls who can't be older than eighteen. They're sporting miniskirts and bikini tops, laughing hysterically as they scroll on their phones.

"Hey, Brett, this is my friend Avery. She has an

appointment with Jesse at 2:00 p.m."

Brett, the man at the front counter, gives me a smile. He looks a little like Ed Sheeran but with a few more tattoos and a nose piercing. I'm not sure what else I would expect. He does work at a tattoo shop.

"Just have a seat, Avery. Jesse's finishing up a piercing in the back room, and then he'll be with you."

I smile, looking to the seating area. The only seat available is the one by the bald, sweaty guy. And I'm not even sure if I could fit one butt cheek on the chair next to him. I decide to just stand.

Jodie flips through some tattoo magazines in the corner as I glance around the shop. The walls are a nice navy blue, a few nautical decorations sprinkled throughout. Nothing over the top. It's simple but nice. I walk over to the other corner, away from the waiting area but still in the front of the shop.

I look up to see a picture of a tattooed man with dark spiky hair and green eyes standing beside a pretty famous singer.

I study the picture, wondering if it's actually him. I embarrassingly reach up to touch the picture, as if I'm Belle studying the magical rose in *Beauty and the Beast*. To be honest, though, I'm also studying the other guy in the picture. He doesn't have as many tattoos as Brett, but full sleeves are visible. His arms ripple beneath his gray T-shirt. I find myself imagining a rock-hard body underneath it all, and then blush. What's wrong with me? I'm acting like a creepy pervert eyeing up the photo. It's like I've never seen an attractive man before. Besides, I've shut that part of my life off right now and—

A voice interrupts my semipsychotic thoughts. It's a voice that sends a weird shiver through my body.

"That's really him," the deep voice says. I turn to see who it is.

It's him, the man from the picture. Not the famous singer, but the tattooed, green-eyed guy. Still, the way I freeze up, you'd think I was face-to-face with a celebrity.

He's smiling at me, studying my reaction. He's got a few days' worth of stubble accenting his jaw. The biceps in the picture seem even more prominent in real life. I find myself studying his arms, the tribal patterns and black-and-white collages causing my gaze to dance up and down his skin.

I finally realize it's been an awkwardly long pause. "Oh, wow. That's neat," I say, mentally scrutinizing my choice of the word "neat." What, am I in sixth grade?

I feel a little hot, sure my cheeks are red.

"I'm Jesse Pearce, owner," he says, reaching out a hand. With the movement of his arm, an oaky cologne scent travels up to my nose, entrancing me even more.

Stop it, Avery, I say to myself. *Get it together.*

"You must be Avery?" he asks as his strong hand shakes mine.

"Yeah, that's me," I say, smiling and laughing nervously.

"She needs rid of the horrific tattoo on her shoulder," Jodie says from behind Jesse, approaching us now. She leans around him to eye me, shaking her head. Jesse turns to face her, and she paints on a smile.

"Well, I'll see what I can do," he says. "Come this way."

I follow Jesse, turning when I realize Jodie isn't coming. "Aren't you coming?"

Jodie winks at me. "You've got this. I'm actually going to head home. Can't wait to see it though."

I pause, eyeing her, but she shoos me on, giving me another wink. Now I shake my head. I see what she's doing here.

"Toodles," she says, breezing out the door as I follow Jesse into a small room down the hallway, a chair sitting in the middle. I get a little nervous now. I'm nervous about the pain, sure.

But I'm also nervous that this man is going to have his hands on me, is going to be staring at my shoulder for a long time.

Which is ludicrous.

"So, let's have a look," Jesse says, super professional as he sits down on the stool in the corner, no hint of sensuality in his voice.

"Okay," I say, grinning. I peel down the strap of my tank top and bra. "Here it is," I say, brushing my hair aside as best as I can as Jesse leans in. I can feel his breath on my neck. I pray I don't visibly shudder.

"Well, this won't be too hard to cover. It's just we're going to have to do a pretty detailed design so the numbers don't show through. Got any ideas?"

I turn to face him, realizing his face is pretty close. Good thing I had some Altoids on the way.

"No?" I say sheepishly, shrugging. "I mean, I've never

really been a tattoo kind of girl. Chris sort of talked me into it. But now I need rid of it."

I wait for Jesse to probe me for information, but he doesn't. "Well, what kind of things do you like?"

I feel like a fool again. I should've been thinking about this. "Well, I like margaritas. I like my mastiff, Henry. Oh, and I love coffee."

He runs a hand through his hair, laughing. "Listen, I know we just met. But I'm going to be honest. You don't seem like the kind of girl to have a margarita glass on your shoulder for all to see. And although my specialty is hyperrealistic portraits, I'm not sure a huge, slobbery mastiff face on your shoulder is going to be exactly sexy. Same with the coffee."

"What's wrong with mastiffs?" I ask, getting a little defensive.

"Nothing at all. I love dogs. I have a bulldog of my own. But I don't think a huge portrait of your dog on your shoulder is going to be something you want, am I wrong?"

He's right, I know. "What's your dog's name?" I ask, not sure why I do.

"Jake."

"Cute. Do you have a picture?"

He nods, pulling out his phone. Jake is the wallpaper. His wrinkly forehead and crooked teeth make me melt. "Adorable. Sorry, I know you're busy. I shouldn't be wasting your time."

"You're not," he replies quickly. "Plus, between you and me, the longer this takes, the higher the chance good old Brett will get stuck doing Mr. Sanders's first tattoo."

"Is that the, um, larger man?"

"The sweating bald guy? Yep. First tattoo. He's an insurance agent from Maine here for the week. He came in today and said he wanted to do something crazy. Pretty sure he's going to pass out."

"Yikes. Okay, then take your time," I say, smiling. I find myself smiling a lot. I probably look like a cheesy infomercial at this point.

"Well, at this rate, it might take five hours to get an idea down," he teases. I just shrug.

"What about a flower or something?"

"That would work. I could make it look good. What's your favorite flower?"

"Lilies, for sure."

"Boom. We've got it. Color preference?"

"Nope. Whatever will look good."

"One more question. And it's a big one. Are you okay with letting me have the creative reins? I'd like for it to be a surprise."

I feel a nervous churning in my stomach. Let this guy I barely know choose my tattoo? I'm going to be stuck with it forever. It's risky.

Still, there's something about the way his voice warms me, something about his green eyes that makes me want to trust him. I stare at him for a moment, knowing it's ridiculous. I shouldn't feel okay with this.

But I do.

So before I can change my mind, I hear my voice confidently saying, "Okay."

And then, before I know it, I'm sitting in the chair, Jesse's two fingers—gloved, of course—are stretching the skin on my shoulder, ready to obliterate Chris's last visible hold on me.

It's silly, but I feel a tear trickle down my cheek at the thought. We've said our goodbyes, and I should be thrilled. The asshole showed his true colors, and I'm lucky to have escaped when I did. I want to be rid of him, want this final part of us stamped out.

Still, I loved him once. There was a time I thought it would be Avery and Chris forever, or at least until death came. I didn't think our lives would be like this, didn't think I'd be nursing a broken heart at the age of twenty-eight.

"You okay? Does it hurt?" Jesse asks tenderly, taking a break from the inking to appraise me.

I swipe at the tear. "I'm okay."

"He's an idiot."

"Who?"

"Whoever the guy was. I know I don't know you, but I know enough to realize he's an absolute moron."

I laugh a little. "Yeah, he was."

"Well, here's the biggest screw you yet, right?"

"Not the biggest one. But a step, I guess."

"Trust me, when I'm done, you won't see him when you look at your shoulder in the mirror."

"I hope so."

"I'm not the best tattoo artist in Ocean City for nothing."

"Mighty confident."

"When it comes to this, you bet."

"Well, I'm glad to be in your hands, then," I say, grimacing a little at the way the words come out.

He just chuckles a little. "Pretty sure Brett's not happy about what's in his hands right now," he says, and I laugh out loud before readjusting and lying back down so he can finish.

In the room next door, we hear Brett calming down the bald man, who is audibly crying.

"Dude, I just drew the first letter. Calm it," we hear Brett say.

"Should you go check on him?" I ask.

"Nah. He's got to learn how to handle the situation. It'll be fine."

For the next hour, though, as Jesse continues erasing the tattoo, the symbol of the old Avery, I hear the earsplitting screams of who I learn is Marvin.

Marvin's tattoo is done before mine, and when he's gone, Brett storms back to the room.

"Excuse me, sorry to interrupt," Brett says.

Jesse puts down the tattoo machine. "Sorry," he says to me.

"No worries."

I turn to see Brett, who is visibly sweating and looks pretty angry.

"I can't believe you didn't even come bail me out."

Jesse chuckles. "Man, you've got to learn somehow."

"But really? My first week and you left me with that guy?"

"You handled it."

"I had to tattoo a heart with his cat's name. On his freaking hip. Seriously. Do you know how unpleasant that was?"

Jesse laughs. "Well, there's a whole gaggle of chicks still waiting for their tattoos in the waiting area. That'll make up for it."

"Wait, are you serious?"

"I'm still finishing up with Avery," Jesse says, nodding toward me. I give a little wave, smiling.

"I'm sure you are," Brett says, stomping off.

Jesse just shakes his head. "Sorry about that. He's having a rough week."

"So it's really his first?"

"First week full-time. He apprenticed with me for the past year and a half. He's just being a bit dramatic."

"Well, not sure if I can blame him after you left him with Marvin."

"Not my fault. This tattoo is supercomplicated, and I have to get it right."

I lean up to look at him, raising an eyebrow. "What, are you doing a portrait of the *Mona Lisa*?"

"You know, Avery, rule one of getting a tattoo—don't piss off the guy with the tattoo equipment who can wreck you for life."

"Can't be any worse than the tattoo I had before," I say.

"Well, you got me there. I'm going to go back to my tattooing now."

I nod, resting my head back down, smiling at the easy banter between us.

If things were different, if Chris hadn't stomped out my belief in love—

Stop it. Stop it, stop it, stop it.

You aren't doing this, I tell myself.

I'm here for a new start, a new sense of independence. I'm here to begin again, to get rid of the old Avery. The old Avery shaped her life around a man. The new Avery won't, especially not a tattoo parlor owner I just met.

Even if he is gorgeous. And funny. And pretty damn sexy.

Shit. Jodie knew exactly what she was doing. I've got to be strong. I can't let it work.

But ten minutes later when he's finished and I get to see the big reveal, tears come to my eyes.

"It's beautiful," I say, meaning it. Gone is the inked heart of my old life, of the man who didn't deserve my heart after all. Gone is the constant reminder of what I had, of who I was.

In its place is a gorgeous, detailed purple lily. It's chic and sophisticated in a way the heart never was.

I turn to face Jesse. Overwhelmed with emotion, I do something highly unprofessional, highly unlike the new Avery.

I wrap my arms around his neck, hugging him tightly, tears flowing onto his black button-up shirt. "I love it so much. Thank you. It's just the new beginning I needed."

He wraps his arms around me, accepting the hug graciously. "You're welcome," he says into my hair, the scent of his oaky cologne again lifting toward me. His warmth wraps around me, and for a moment, it feels good to be in his arms.

Then I get a grip. I don't even know this man. I'm in an intimate hug I initiated with my tattoo artist. He probably thinks I'm a stalker, a psycho, or both.

"Sorry," I say, pulling away, tucking my hair behind my ear. "I just got carried away."

"It's okay," he says, showing his gorgeous teeth as he slides his hands in his pockets. "Glad you like it. I'm here to make my customers happy."

Something about the way it rolls off his tongue—or perhaps it's my horny mind wandering—makes me tingle inside a bit. I have a feeling he could make someone very happy in all the right ways.

I shake my head. "Um, okay. Do I pay out front?" I ask, trying to bring some semblance of a business relationship back.

"It's on the house," Jesse says, brushing aside my wallet.

"What? No way. Not happening."

"No, seriously. I know what it's like to need a new start. I do. So please. Just here, give my card to friends. Tell people I'm the best tattoo artist around. That's how you can pay me."

"I can't. I can't accept this."

"You absolutely can."

The prideful part of me wants to fight, to insist on paying him. Instead, though, feeling like a new woman, I smile and say, "Thank you." I take a handful of cards and head out the door as Jesse walks back toward Brett, probably going to bail him out of the room of shrieking divas.

I want to turn around so badly when I get to the door, just to see those green eyes one more time, but I don't.

This is so stupid. I'm not going to see him again. I got my new tattoo, I'm ready to start over, and I've accomplished one of my goals.

As I walk toward home, I notice I have a little more bounce in my step. Despite the burning sensation on my shoulder and the pain, I feel better than I have in months.

I tell myself it's the new tattoo, and not the man who gave it to me.

Chapter Six

"Gorgeous."

"It is pretty nice," I say, admiring my new ink. I'm standing in my room glancing in the mirror above my dresser. Jodie's in the doorway.

"I'm not talking about the tattoo," she says. I look over in time to see her signature wink.

"Don't," I say, knowing what's coming.

"Don't what? Come on. He had his hands all over your shoulders. Don't tell me you didn't get a little hot and bothered. He's damn gorgeous."

I feel my face redden. I put the bandage back in place, and readjust the strap on my tank top gingerly. I head toward the kitchen, brushing by Jodie to get a bottle of water from the fridge. Looking into the living room, I see that Henry's dead asleep on the sofa, drooling, Sebastian sleeping in the crook of his leg. I smile, but Jodie's words quickly melt it off my face.

"At least admit he's pretty cute."

"Why? Why does it matter, Jodie? I told you. I'm done with men. Not interested. Been there, done that, and been burned."

"Listen. I'm not saying marry the guy. But I am saying the best way to get over what Chris did to you is to find someone else. Have some fun. Jesse could be fun for you. God knows he could stand to live a little, too."

Grabbing my water from the fridge, I take a seat at the kitchen island. "What do you mean?"

Jodie stands across from me, leaning on the counter. "Rumor has it he's had a rough few years."

"Really? He seemed okay to me. Joking and laughing."

"Of course. Because you're beautiful. Plus, I told him all about you when I called."

"You didn't."

"You really think I sent you to J & J's because of their tattooing skills?" She rolls her eyes, smiling. "You said you came here to break away from your old life. What better way than a supersexy tattooed hunk who has nice, strong hands and a sense of humor? He's attractive, he's business savvy, and he's super nice. I knew he'd be just the thing to get your mind off old what's-his-name. And I knew you'd never pursue it. You just needed a little shove, right?"

I'm appalled. I exhale audibly. "Glad to know I trusted you. So he could've been the worst tattoo artist ever and you'd have sent me?"

She shrugs. "I mean, relax. He isn't the worst, obviously. But hell, even if he had jittery hands, I'd probably take the

LINDSAY DETWILER

risk to have those sexy hands all over me. Admit it. It was heavenly."

I dodge her question, shaking my head. "Maybe you and Jesse should date," I say. "You two would be a good pair."

She laughs. "Please. Not my type."

"Why not?"

"I don't know. He's just too... serious for me? Too responsible, maybe? I need a wilder man."

"You said he'd be perfect to help me live it up."

"Yeah, he would. But you're a little more... shall I say, traditional than me?"

"So you're saying I'm boring?"

"No. I'm just saying you and Jesse would be a good match. You're both responsible and mature but you need to spice things up. You need to break free from the past. I think you could do that together."

"And how do you know so much about Jesse? You must've had quite the heart-to-heart during your tattoo session."

Jodie's smile widens. "I mean, we did talk a little. But I mostly know him because Brett and I banged a few times last summer."

My jaw drops open. Jodie doesn't look bothered or embarrassed in the slightest. She just shrugs. "A girl has her needs," she says.

I do the only thing I can.

I laugh.

"What happened?"

"He wasn't my type, either. Brett was a little too giggly

in bed. He had this weird habit of—"

"Enough," I interrupt, tossing my hands up in front of me. "Please. I don't need to know any more details."

"See what I mean? You're very straitlaced, conservative. Jesse said the same thing when we were talking about it during my tattoo."

"You talked about it during your tattoo? While Brett was there?"

"No. He was off that day. And why not? It's not like I'm embarrassed. Why are we so closed-off about sex? We're young. We should be exploring, having fun."

"So your type is what, a sex addict? A swinger?"

She finds this uproariously funny. "I don't know about that. But maybe just not someone who is so uptight. Someone who isn't afraid to have fun. And being rich might not be a bad thing, either, you know? I'll take a sugar daddy, maybe."

I laugh a little. "You're ridiculous."

"But at least I'm honest. Unlike some people who won't admit it when they find a man worth letting go of a few principles for."

"Okay, look. He seems like a nice guy. And yeah, he's mildly attractive. But I told you. I'm here for me, not for love or even lust. Plus, it's not like I'll see him again anyway. It was a one-time thing. I'm not planning on getting a full sleeve done or anything."

Jodie sort of skips toward the living room to get her laptop, probably to work on her book. "You never know," she yells over her shoulder, giggling a little bit.

"What's that supposed to mean?" I ask, worried about what she has up her sleeve.

"Oh, I think you might see him again. It's a small town," she says, scooching Henry over just a smidgen so she can sit down with the two laziest animals I've ever seen.

"It's not really a small town," I retort.

"Don't worry. You'll see him." She turns toward me and winks conspiratorially, but I just shake my head.

It doesn't matter, though. She's wrong. She's just excited to play matchmaker. Nothing will come of it.

And even if it does, I'll make sure to stomp out the fire before it incinerates me this time.

I head to my room to take a nap and think about how crazy life is… but how crazy simple it is, too.

Chapter Seven

The days drift by, and I fall into a routine, against my desires. Work in the evenings. Walks with Henry in the mornings, fighting him all the way to get off the couch. Agonizing phone conversations with my mother on Sunday afternoons. Wild nights out on Friday or Saturday, depending on Jodie's and my schedules. Coffee with Jodie in the morning before she plasters herself to her computer to finish her latest manuscript. Groceries on Thursday afternoon.

Life is getting pretty predictable already.

So, on a Tuesday morning, after our morning coffee and gossip session, I ask Jodie where the nearest craft store is.

"I think there's one on Twenty-Ninth and Baltimore. What do you need?"

"Canvases. And some paints. An easel, too."

"Painting? I mean, I know you like to sketch in your spare time, but I didn't know you were into painting."

When we're hanging out at home and Jodie's writing, sometimes I break out my sketchbook, getting some of my frustrations and feelings out in random drawings. Jodie insists I'm pretty good. I've never told her, though, that I also have a thing for painting—mostly because I didn't see a need to. It's been years since I've busted out a brush and canvas.

I shrug and glance at her. "I used to be really into painting. A long time ago in high school, I used to love painting scenery. I took a few art classes and even won a few contests. I had my own mini studio set up in my room."

"What happened?" she asks, raising her second cup of coffee to her pink lips.

I shrug. "I don't know. I guess I knew art was never going to be my career, so I just kind of put my focus on other things."

"Well, awesome. Get out there and get some painting done. You could be the next Picasso or something."

"Um, he was more abstract."

"Okay, then you'll be the next... who is big on scenery painting? Oh, screw it. You'll be the next Avery Johannas. Johannas even sounds like a painter."

"There was a Johannes Vermeer, but it's pronounced differently. And spelled differently. Obviously."

"Never heard of him. Obviously," she says, flipping her hair, shrugging. Sebastian meows at her feet, and she quickly scooches off her stool to go and give him some food. I finish my coffee, drag Henry outside to pee, and then grab my sunglasses off the counter, the craft store my next stop.

***

An hour later, I've found myself a piece of beach back

from the sunbathers. It's not as early as I would like—the sun has already been up for hours. Tomorrow, I'll try to get out here earlier, if I can drag my butt out of bed.

Some kids play volleyball on a patch of sand thirty feet in front of my easel. I'm pretty sure they're going to spike a ball and destroy my carefully organized painting station. Nonetheless, I can't wipe the smile off my face. As my brush grazes the canvas, I'm happy to say I like what I see. More than that, I like the feel of the brush in my hand, the freedom of not having a plan as I paint the world as I see it. For once, I don't have to worry about how I'm supposed to see things. The brush in my hand doesn't lie.

"Looks great," a voice says behind me, and I involuntarily shudder. Luckily, I'd been studying the horizon and not painting. I turn to see the face belonging to the voice.

"Sorry," he says. "Didn't mean to mess up your groove."

Green eyes stare back at me, and suddenly, I feel myself readjusting my bangs, smooching my lips together to make sure my lip gloss is evenly applied. I get mad at myself for this, but I can't help it.

He was gorgeous in a button-up and jeans in the tattoo parlor.

He's unforgivingly, overtly sexy standing shirtless beside me now. My gaze wanders lower and lower to his tanned six-pack, studying the tattoos smattered all over his body. There are a decent number of images, as one would expect from a tattoo artist. Still, they're tasteful, tactfully placed, not over the top. After all, they still allow an unblocked view of his rock-hard body, including those delicious-looking abs.

"I was out for a run and saw you over here. Thought I'd swing by and see how your tattoo is doing. Is it healing okay? Glad to see you've got it covered. Direct sunlight isn't good for healing, like we talked about."

I avert my eyes back to my canvas, now feeling self-conscious about my obvious staring and the fact he's seeing my painting.

"It's fine. Looks great. I love it," I say, the choppy phrases the best I can do.

"Didn't know you like to paint. This looks awesome."

So far, I only have the sky and some of the water done. It's not really impressive, but I appreciate his kind words. They soften my nerves a bit. "Thanks. I haven't done this in forever."

"Doesn't look that way. You're really good, Avery."

"I don't know about that."

"I do. I tried painting once, and trust me, it looked nothing like this. It's beautiful."

"Hey, don't discount what you do. You're such an amazing artist. To be able to do all of that drawing and shading, you have to have skill."

"It's different, completely different. I always wished I could paint. Maybe sometime you could teach me," he says, and I nod. He looks a little nervous now, like he's not sure how I'll respond.

"Yeah, that would be great. Don't know how helpful I'd be."

"And I'm not sure how good I'd be. Maybe we could get lunch or something afterward, as payment for dealing with my horrific painting."

I hesitate. The way he says lunch conjures images of a date. A part of me, the part still admiring his green eyes and the peripheral view of his abs, wants to say, "Hell yes, sign me up."

But the other part of me, the rational part of me, thinks, "No way."

Chris was a gorgeous man, too. I've fallen for sexy before, and look how it turned out. I don't even know Jesse, not really. I can't risk getting involved.

"Jesse," I say, biting my lip for a moment because this is about to get awkward. "I'd love to help you with your painting and all. But, just so we're clear, it would be as friends. I'm not interested in dating."

He doesn't leave any pause, any moment of silence. "No, no. Of course. I'm not interested either. It would be a completely platonic situation. Seriously."

I study him for a moment. On one hand, he was quick to answer. I believe him. He's not interested in anything beyond friendship, which is a relief.

But standing by my canvas, the summer sun causing sweat to bead on my forehead, I wonder why his words sting like salt water in an open wound.

He's not interested. Like, not at all.

It shouldn't bother me. It shouldn't surprise me. Why the hell would a man like Jesse be interested in some boring, lame woman like me? No man like him is going to want a twentysomething divorcee who is looking for a wild time painting canvases on the beach.

I'm glad I don't have to worry about crossing a line. He's not interested, which makes the temptation easier to resist.

Still, the words play over and over in my head, long after he's said his farewell and run off down the beach.

He's not interested. There's no chance.

Those eyes will only be looking at me platonically, and those abs will never be mine to touch.

I finish my painting before heading back to the apartment to get ready for work. There's a little less bounce in my brush, a little less life in my strokes. When I'm done, the painting looks real enough, but it's rigid and too realistic. There's no emotion, no life in it.

It's missing something.

***

"Shit, the cash register isn't working again. Now I have to do math. I'm a writer, not a freaking statistician." Jodie is holding her head by the cash register, panic on her face as she studies her tablet.

"Let me see it," I say reaching for the paper. After a quick mental calculation, I tell her, "The total would be thirty-six dollars and forty-two cents."

"Okay, Einstein, slow down already."

I smile. "I was an accountant, remember?" I rush off toward the table of college-aged kids waiting for their greasy fried foods, feeling much more confident than I did when I first started.

This waitressing thing is coming along. I only dropped one drink all week, managed to get some decent tips, and even remembered to smile. Most of all, I'm actually liking the work. It's still stressful as hell, probably more stressful than working at the firm. I go home with an aching back and feet when I leave, and sometimes the customers' attitudes are a bit salty. Still, there's something special about having Lysander, Jodie, and even Reed to laugh with during cleanup.

Max, another waiter who is working to make money for college, brushes by me. "Family emergency, Avery. Can you get table sixteen?"

"Yeah, no problem," I yell over my shoulder as he rushes toward the door. I turn to see table sixteen in the back corner.

I freeze. Good thing there isn't a drink in my hand, or I'd have to up the dropped-drinks count.

It's him. Green eyes. Jesse.

"Shit," I mutter, and the table of rowdy twentysomethings look at me in surprise before laughing. I rush back toward the kitchen.

"What's wrong? You look like you've seen Shakespeare's ghost," Jodie says.

"Worse."

"What?"

"Max asked me to cover table sixteen."

"So what?" Jodie asks, stretching her neck to peer at table sixteen. She turns back to me, not in horror, but in delight, clapping her hands. "Oh, of course. It's Tuesday. It's Jesse's night."

"What are you talking about?"

"Every Tuesday when he comes in, he sits at table sixteen. We save it for him. It's his thing."

I raise an eyebrow. "You're not lying to me, are you?"

"Of course not. What, did you think he was stalking you?"

I sheepishly avert my eyes. "Of course not." I sort of did, which is embarrassing now. How full of myself am I?

"Listen, I don't blame you for wishing Mr. Ink was stalking you. Now get over there and serve him." She winks coyly before rushing back to her side of the restaurant, leaving me with abnormal heart palpitations, sweaty palms, and a sudden frustration for my job.

I calmly walk over to the table. "Hey," I say. "What can I get you?"

"Hey, Avery. How's the tattoo?"

"Fine. No changes since this morning," I reply, smiling.

He tousles his hair with a hand, seemingly wishing he could take back his question. He seems a little nervous, too, judging by his tapping foot and pinker than normal cheeks. "Right. Dumb question. Anyway, I'll have my usual, the burger and fried pickles."

I involuntarily grimace. "Fried pickles? We have those?"

"Yeah, they're awesome. You've never had them?"

"Never. Ew."

"Okay, give me two orders of them, in that case."

I shake my head. "Whatever you want." I put my pen down and look down at him. "Be right back."

Over the next fifteen minutes, I wait on my other seven tables, rushing around delivering drinks, answering questions about the restaurant to newcomers, saying a prayer to Shakespeare's spirit that table fourteen will leave already when I see them taking bets on who can flip the water glass over without spilling it, and trying not to trip.

I also find my gaze wandering to table sixteen, to my chagrin.

Jesse sits there, arms crossed, his back leaning against the wooden booth seat. He stares out the window directly in front of him, the darkness of the summer night probably not giving him much to see. He looks peaceful but also wistful in some way. I can't help but wonder what his story is. He's friendly and warm, but there's a deepness to him. I see it in those eyes when he looks at me. He's masking something, covering something. I remember what Jodie said about him having a rough few years, and I wonder if her words are even truer than she realizes.

When Jesse's order is up, I grab it and deliver.

"Here you go."

"Have a seat," Jesse says. I turn back and see my waiting tables.

"I can't. I have tables to wait on."

"I asked Lysander if you could take your break now."

I look over to the bar in time for Lysander to wink at me. Is everyone here conspiring to match me up? I know the answer without even asking.

"Okay." I clumsily climb into the seat across from Jesse, wiping my brow with the back of my hand, feeling self-conscious about the sight and smell of me. Waitressing is never glamorous, and those women in the movies who look gorgeous while doing it quite simply don't exist.

Jesse slides the second basket of fried pickles across

the table. "Try one."

I grimace. "What? No way. You ordered these for me?"

He shrugs. "Every woman deserves to try fried pickles in her lifetime."

I want to argue and say no, disgusting. I want to talk about how it's unprofessional or how it's just gross or how it's too high in calories. But then I remember my vow to break away from the past.

So I take a deep breath as if I'm preparing for a marathon or a root canal, and I pick up the greasy, crispy pickle.

I mentally count to three before shoving it in my mouth.

And I'm shocked. It's freaking good. Like so good, I finish it and reach for another.

"Oh, look at that. I do know what I'm talking about," he says, shoving a fried pickle in his own mouth.

"Okay, so they're not so bad," I say, reaching for another and smiling.

"That's what I thought. They were always my dad's favorite. When he first ordered them, I gave him the same look you gave me. But I came around."

I chew up my fried pickle, hoping there isn't any in my teeth. Somehow, though, Jesse doesn't seem like the guy who would care, even if I did. He's right across from me, chomping away like this is an everyday occurrence for us. He's relaxed and comfortable. It makes me feel the same.

"Does your dad live around here?"

"No. Dad died about ten years ago now."

"Oh my God, I'm so sorry." Great. Bringing down the mood over fried pickles. My forte.

"It's okay. I brought him up."

There is now a stiff silence. I don't know if I should ask more questions or leave it go. I opt for the second choice just because I don't really know what to say.

"So tell me about you," he says, probably feeling the awkwardness of the silence too. "Where did you grow up?"

"I'm from a town just outside Pittsburgh, Pennsylvania. My parents own a CPA firm there, where I worked."

"What made you decide to come here? Was it him?" He gestures toward my shoulder, and I know exactly what he's getting at.

"Pretty much. I needed a new life. I was feeling suffocated. When my marriage fell apart, I decided to do what I'd always wanted to do but didn't have the courage to. I picked up and moved here, wanting to try a new life. Does that seem crazy?"

"Not at all." He grins. "I basically did the same thing ten years ago. Not because of a broken marriage, but still. Sometimes those big life moments make you realize you aren't living the life you want."

"Exactly. It was a tough time, but I'm sort of realizing it might not have been the worst thing. I'm finding a new groove here, and I'm happy."

"Glad to hear it. Listen, if you ever need anything, just let me know. I know it can be fun uprooting your life, but it can be scary too."

"Thanks. I appreciate it." I smile at him, seeing the genuine kindness in his eyes. He's not trying to make a move—or stalk me. He's just a really nice guy. Behind his stoic, professional attitude is a genuinely good guy who gets where I'm coming from.

At least it seems that way over our fried pickle encounter.

"Well, I better get back to work," I say. "Thanks for the pickles."

"Anytime. Really," he says, smiling as I scooch out of the booth.

As I'm walking away, I stop and turn. "Maybe we could set up a painting lesson soon?" I ask, letting him know I haven't forgotten.

"Yeah, I'm game."

"Great. See you around."

"See you around."

I saunter back to the kitchen, Jodie's grin huge. "Painting lesson? Sounds intimate," she says, winking.

"Stop, you creepy eavesdropper. How did you even hear that?"

"I have my methods," she says, winking again.

"Well, it's not like that. We're just friends."

"With benefits, I hope."

"You're crazy." I head over to table twelve to get them started with a round of drinks.

The rest of the night is pretty uneventful. We only have one near-fight at the bar area that Lysander has to break up. I don't drop any food or mess up any orders. Jodie even manages to give her number to a cute guy in a business suit who is visiting from Detroit for the weekend.

For one seemingly regular night, all is well in life.

Chapter Eight

"So, did you set up your painting lesson yet? Any new brushstrokes?" Reed asks as Lysander and Jodie huddle around me. It's Wednesday night, and we're closing the place up after a pretty intense karaoke night.

"Oh, stop. We're just friends."

"So boring. Come on. The man is gorgeous. If he was gay, I might have taken a crack at him," Reed says. Lysander groans. "Before you, of course."

"I'm not looking for love. Really."

"What woman comes to the beach, gives up her old boring life, and swears off men? Stop being so conservative. Loosen up, girl," Lysander says, nudging me.

"Yes. Get your party on."

"I've been partying. We go out on weekends sometimes."

"Yeah, and you have a few martinis if we're lucky. Plus, you turn down every guy we send your way," Reed complains. This discussion is starting to get an intervention vibe.

"You did come here to have fun, didn't you?" Lysander asks.

"I did, within reason. I don't know what kind of girl you think I was, but trust me, even before the whole matrimony and mortgage thing, I was never quite a wild one. I didn't come here to go crazy, guys. I just came here for a fresh start, for a life that was a little less… scripted."

"You're still being boring," Reed adds.

"Agreed," Lysander seconds.

Jodie, who has been uncharacteristically quiet, studies me. "I think I know the problem," she says, putting a finger up as if she's just had a truly genius thought. It terrifies me.

"What?" I ask.

"It's the hair."

I raise an eyebrow, self-consciously putting a hand to the ends of my brown, shoulder-length hair.

"Excuse me?" I ask. "What's wrong with my hair?"

"It's boring. Come on, Avery. A brown lob. It screams middle-aged married woman who is off the market."

"It doesn't. My hairdresser said it looked chic. And it's not boring brown. It's a warm chocolate brown. She said it complemented my complexion."

"Now that you mention it, Jo, you're right. You're totally right. It's the hair. It doesn't scream 'come hither.' It screams librarian or middle-aged soccer mom… and not in a sexy way."

"Are soccer moms ever sexy?" Lysander asks, and Reed shrugs.

"Guys, ouch. Just kill my ego."

"Your hair is doing that for you," Jodie adds. "I should've thought about this before. A woman looking for a new life needs a new haircut. It's as simple as that."

"I don't know. My hair's worked up until this point. I don't know if I want to change it."

"Come on, darling, listen to Jodie. Lysander and I know this fabulous guy, seriously. He's a miracle worker. He'll have you prancing out of his shop looking like Renee Zellweger or Kate Beckinsale. Seriously."

"Isn't it time for a change?" Lysander reasons. Again, I'm feeling the intervention-like vibes creep in.

Still, running a hand through my hair, I admit it's a little exciting. Maybe they're right. Maybe it's time for a change.

With a sigh of resignation, I cave to the hair intervention. "What the hell. Get me an appointment."

The three of them jump up and down like they've just won the lottery.

"You guys, I appreciate your help. But can I ask something? What did you used to do before you had me as your little pet project?"

Jodie examines the ends of her hair now. "Um, well, let's see. We gossiped more about Alex, the weekend cook, and tried to guess his sexual orientation."

"We went through a brief tennis phase," Lysander adds.

"We tried fixing Jo up with every man in a six-mile radius," Reed says.

I look at them all, shaking my head. "You three are unbelievable. Seriously. But I love you."

"Let me ask you this. What did you do without us?"

Reed asks now, smiling.

"I think I just sat around wondering what it would be like to have a group of friends like you."

"That's pathetic," Jodie says, grinning to soften the blow. "Thank God we came into your life, or you'd be one of those creepy cat ladies sitting around knitting sweaters and watching game shows. We got to you just in time."

"Give us a few months. You won't even recognize your old self," Lysander says. "Except the good parts, of course."

"I'm starting to worry there aren't good parts."

"Honey, you're gorgeous and sweet. You're supersmart. You just need a little nudge to be the best version of yourself. You've spent too much time being his other half. Now you've got to learn how to be just Avery, how to stand on your own feet." Reed isn't smiling or laughing. It's an unusually serious moment from him.

I nod at the truth in his words. He gets it. He gets me.

And although sometimes I wonder if this is the life I'm meant to find, lately, it seems more and more like I'm right where I belong.

***

I think I might puke up my Captain Crunch any second. Seriously. I've never been this nervous, not even on my wedding day.

"One," Alexander counts out loud with as much drama as a person could possibly muster. He's leaning down in front of me, one hand on either side of me as he holds the chair. I take a deep breath. This is it.

"Two," Jodie says, standing right beside him, clapping dramatically.

"I hope I don't regret this," I say, interrupting the countdown.

Jodie convinced me to live a little and let her and Alexander pick my hairstyle… without me seeing it. I've been in Alexander's salon, Beach Babes, for hours. My hair has been pretreated, colored, highlighted, washed, dried, cut, fluffed, and styled. My neck hurts from leaning back in the sink so many times, and I'm starving. Beauty is pain and all that—but I'm ready to see the results.

But I'm not. I'm terrified to see what these two concocted. From Jodie's over-the-top personality to the fact Alexander is sporting a magenta mohawk, I have no idea what to expect.

"Three," Alexander says, whirling me around.

There is a long moment of silence as I stare in the mirror, my eyes adjusting to the "new" me. I'm not really sure what to think. I'm speechless, not out of shock, just out of "what the hell happened?"

My hair's a little shorter and now super layered. It looks like Alexander razored pieces into it to give me the edgy vibe. The chocolate brown is now a bright, bright blonde. I've never been a blonde, so I'm not sure what to think.

The most shocking thing, though, is the hot-pink streak on my left side. I look like a rocker without the charisma.

"Do you love it? Isn't it great?" Jodie says.

I'm not thinking about love right now, though. I'm thinking about how my mom would react if she could see this. I'm thinking about how unprofessional I look, how no reputable CPA firm would ever hire me. I'm thinking of all these practical reasons why I should make Alexander color my hair the flat brown it used to be, and run out of here.

Instead, I shove the practical Avery thoughts aside. I look at myself, really look at myself.

I grin. "I actually love it. It's fun."

I mean it, running a hand through the pink streak and fluffing the layers. A smile spreads on my face, and I can't help but feel radiant. It's a new side of me. It's the side of Avery I always wanted to be but couldn't—because of Chris, because of my job, because of who I decided to be in order for society to approve.

But this pink/blonde-haired Avery looks like fun. I flip my hair in a sassy way, feeling a confidence I have never had.

Alexander claps wildly, apparently happy all his hard work paid off. I sashay to the counter, leave him a huge tip on my card, and turn to Jodie.

"Do you need to get back to your writing?" I ask, knowing she's under a publishing deadline.

"I mean, technically yeah. But I could be persuaded to shirk off my responsibilities for a while longer. What do you have in mind?"

"Shopping. These clothes just aren't quite right anymore," I say, looking down to appraise my trouser jeans and button-up pink cardigan. "I need some help finding some twentysomething clothes that say fun instead of practical."

Jodie actually lets out a squeal. "Yes! I was hoping you'd say that. Shopping spree. I could use a new pair of heels, now that you mention it. Let's go. I know some great places."

We spend the next few hours trying on all kinds of styles, laughing, and swiping our plastic way too much. Still, it feels so good to let go.

It feels so good to come into my own, I think in bed that night, flipping my hair one last time before drifting off to sleep beside Henry, and kiss the librarian, soccer mom Avery goodbye.

***

"Are you sure this isn't too revealing?" I ask, eyeing the neon pink halter and tan shorts Jodie put me in this morning.

"Honey, you're twenty-eight and you've got a body like a celebrity. There is no such thing as too revealing."

"But I don't want him to think I'm trying to impress him. This is just—"

"A painting lesson," Jodie says, mocking me. "I know. You've told me ten times. Who are you trying to convince here—me or you?"

"I'm serious. I don't want him getting the wrong idea."

"I think he's going to get all sorts of right ideas," she says, winking as always. I shake my head. "Now get out of here and go to your painting lesson. You're on the schedule at two, remember? I have to get my manuscript finished. My agent didn't buy my excuse that new shoes were an absolute necessity yesterday."

I gather up the canvases and supplies, heading out the door toward my spot.

I'd called J & J's last night, feeling bold enough to set up a painting lesson. I felt like I owed him after the pickle scenario.

Okay, let's be real. It's not about fried pickles. It's about me wanting to see him again, despite my best effort to deny it.

Jesse was up for the whole painting gig and promised to meet me here.

Sure enough, as I round the corner past the beach grasses to the spot we've picked, he's standing there in a muscle shirt and board shorts, Ray Ban sunglasses completing the vibe.

"Hey," I say as he rushes to help me carry all the painting equipment.

He just stares and smiles, taking some things out of my arms. "Your hair. It's awesome. Wow," he says, flashing those killer teeth.

"Oh, thanks. Just wanted a change." I automatically run a hand through it. I need to stop it. I hate girls who are always flipping their hair.

"It looks amazing. Wow." He keeps staring as if he literally can't take his eyes off me. I feel awkward, not really used to this sort of attention. Back home, when I tried to do something different with my hair—which usually meant going one shade darker than usual—Chris never even noticed. In fairness, this is a bit more drastic, but still. It's good to be noticed.

"So, are you ready to paint?" I ask.

"Yeah, let's do it."

I start standing up the easels and placing the canvases on them. I order Jesse to get the palettes ready to go.

"Beach scene?" I ask, and he nods. He's still looking at me, and my stomach flutters under his gaze.

"Okay, I've already prepped the canvas, so here we go," I say as I find the correct brushes we need first and show Jesse how to hold it properly. He copies my moves. I feel pressure now to do a good job.

I lead him through a few basic brush strokes. A compliant student, he listens to my every word, mimicking me when he can.

After a half hour, I appraise our progress.

Jesse's looks nothing like mine, despite his best efforts. It's muddy and murky. It looks more like a horror scene than a cheery beach scene.

I scratch my head, forgetting there is paint on my hands.

"Oh, man, you got blue in your hair."

"Shit," I say, holding my hands out, not sure what to do.

He laughs. "You're really taking this edgy thing pretty far, huh? How about some green on this side," he says, pretending to hold his brush near my hair.

I scream, slapping the brush away. He laughs as I dash away from him through the sand, inspired by the moment. He chases me across the beach, laughing like a five-year-old. Despite my initial annoyance, I give way to laughter too.

When he finally stops and puts his brush back in the brush holder, he sighs.

"I don't think I have the knack for painting," he says, studying his canvas. I approach him, cocking my head at his painting, trying to find anything positive to hang on to.

"I mean, it's... different."

"It sucks."

I look at him to judge whether or not I can be honest. I decide he can take it. "Yeah, it's pretty bad. Sorry."

He shrugs. "I think it's just the teacher. She's a little strange, you know? And, between you and me, I think she just brought me here to show me up."

I gasp in mock horror. "This was your idea," I say, pointing at him.

"Please. After those pickles, you practically begged me to come here. You're just hoping I buy you some more."

"I have an in with the restaurant. Pretty sure I could snag some without you."

"Yeah, but they're not the same if you don't eat them with a tattooed, hilarious guy like me."

"Full of ourselves much?" I tease. I shake my head, looking off toward the surf. It's early enough that the beachgoers aren't quite filling the sand yet. A few rogue chairs line the water's edge, and a few kids play in the water.

Feeling spontaneous, I decide to abandon our painting station. "Come on," I say, tugging on Jesse's hand. After I do, I feel a little self-conscious. *Don't give him the wrong idea,* I think to myself, yanking my hand out of his. I don't want him to think I'm making a move.

I dash down the beach, and he follows. The July sun is already warming the sand—in a few hours, it'll be scorching hot. The wind whips my paint-streaked hair every which way, and I'm sure it doesn't quite look like one of the women on *Baywatch.* I feel like a five-year-old as I gleefully skip toward the waves.

When we reach the water, I plunk my feet in and scream.

"Damn, it's cold."

"You haven't been down to the water yet?" Jesse asks, standing beside me.

"Nope. Been too busy setting up my life."

"You're a terrible beach girl, you know? What, you've been here like a month and you haven't been down here? What kind of person spontaneously picks up and moves here… but doesn't go to the beach?"

I grin. "A boring one, I guess. I'm still new to this whole spontaneous thing."

"Well, at least you're getting better at it. God, when I moved here, the first thing I did was come down to the water. I didn't even have a place to live yet, but here I was, feet in the water."

"How old were you when you moved here?" I ask.

"Eighteen."

"Did you come alone?" I ask, feeling like the freeing breeze and lapping water make a perfect, soothing backdrop for nosy questions.

"Yep. Just me."

I take in the sight of the sun beaming over the water, not really sure where to go with this conversation next.

Jesse picks it up for me, perhaps the serene setting prompting him to open up a bit. "My dad loved this place. We didn't have much money growing up. He was a mechanic, and his income wasn't the highest. Still, he would save and save so he could bring me here for a week every other summer. I looked forward to that week for two full years. I would put every penny, every nickel I could find in our beach jar so we could come back. I guess his parents always brought him here, and he loved the place. I fell in love with it, too. There's just something powerful about standing here, feeling so small. There's something magical about the excitement and energy on the boardwalk, yet the peace you find here."

A wave sends me slightly off-kilter, and I lean into Jesse's shoulder. He keeps staring into the ocean, and I smile, happy he's opening up.

"What about your mom?" I venture. "Did she like it here?"

I look up in time to see his jaw clench. I wish I could take the words back, wish I hadn't usurped this peaceful moment for him. I get the sense that opening up isn't his strong suit.

"I wouldn't know. She abandoned us when I was just two. Left my dad for a man she met at work. Picked up and took off. She cleaned out my dad's savings and checking accounts, left him high and dry with a two-year-old. Never heard from her again."

"I'm so sorry," I say, gently touching his arm. He looks down at me, shrugging.

"It's okay. Dad gave me a good life."

"So when you came here, did you have favorite places? Did you have a routine?"

Jesse's grin is back. I've asked a good question.

"Dad liked to spend as much time on the sand as possible. We'd get up at six in the morning to come and claim our spot, always as close to the water as possible. We'd spend

Inked Hearts

the day here, playing in the sand, building sand castles, boogie boarding when I got older. There's a small sub shack a few blocks back from the boardwalk. Around noon, we'd head back and get sandwiches before coming back out for the afternoon."

"Sounds amazing."

"It was." He pauses, and I turn to see a wistful look in his eyes as he rubs the stubble on his chin, looking out into the vast horizon. He turns to look at me, smiling. "We also loved Midsummer Nights, believe it or not. On Tuesday of the week we were here, Dad would take me there. It was when Lysander's mom Janet was running the place. Dad would always get a Love-in-Idleness and let me have a sip."

"You rebel," I say, winking.

"That's me all right."

"Is that why you still come every Tuesday?"

"You bet. It's the same booth Dad and I would sit at."

I want to know more. I want to know more about Jesse's life, about how he ended up here, about his dad. But I also don't want to push too far. I don't want to scare him away.

"Well, I guess I should head back and check on Henry," I say, sad to end this moment between us. I glance at the water one last time before stepping back, my toes back in the dry sand instead of the cold, salty water.

"Do you work today?" Jesse asks.

"At two. I get done at nine, though."

Jesse kicks up some water, hands in his pockets. Finally, he looks at me, those green eyes piercing into mine. "So, Jake's been a little lonely lately because I've been working

85

more hours at the shop. What do you think about going for a walk tonight on the beach, after you're done with work? You could bring Henry so Jake would have a new friend."

"Are dogs allowed on the beach?"

Jesse smiles. "I'm a rebel, remember? Of course not. But it'll be dark. No one will say anything, especially not to a lady walking a mastiff."

"I'll warn you, Henry is pretty lazy, so I'm not sure how long the walk will be."

"Jake's ten pounds overweight. Pretty sure he'll be okay with a short walk."

"Sounds like they might be a perfect pair. I mean as friends, of course."

"Of course," Jesse says, grinning. "So how about 10:00 p.m.? Does that work for you?"

"Sounds great. I'll meet you outside Midsummer Nights?"

"Perfect," he says, and we head back to clean up the painting lesson gone wrong. As we trash the canvases and clean up my easel, though, I can't help but think that in some ways, the painting lesson might have gone terribly right.

Chapter Nine

"This seems like an absolutely horrible idea," I say, nursing my cup of coffee as I force my feet through the sand. The beach is still hazy, the sun not even up yet. Jodie, of course, is practically skipping through the sand, her neon yellow workout tank way too loud for this time.

"It's going to be great! New day, new you. You'll thank me."

"It's way too early."

"Not my fault you had a steamy, late-night date."

I brush my bangs out of my eyes as I grin. I can't even deny it.

Last night with Jesse was wonderful.

Okay, let's back up. It's not like anything crazy wonderful happened—there was no wild time on the sand, which is perfectly okay with me. Sex on the beach never did seem appealing.

Not that I would want that anyway, I remind myself, wiping the smirk off my face. It's just my drowsiness and the early hour that has me thinking crazy, has me reminiscing about last night like a love-drunk teenager.

There was simply a moonlight walk, the tide lapping against our toes as Henry and Jake met for the first time. As our dogs greeted each other in the typical ways, Jesse and I ambled down the beach, talking about the basics, covering all of the favorite color and favorite holiday and favorite everything kind of talk.

As friends, of course.

"It wasn't a date," I argue, still clinging to my cup of coffee like it's my life source.

"Yeah, okay. Because Jesse meets with tons of girls with Jake on the beach. You know, hanging by the sea late at night, languidly strolling down the beach... nope, nothing romantic there." Jodie rolls her eyes, smiling in her endearing way. I scowl back at her.

"Our dogs were sniffing each other's butts. So no, not quite romantic. Plus, Jake tried to hump Henry."

Jodie squeals with laughter. "How did that even work? Never mind, I don't need the visual. Anyway, maybe you two could take a hint." She makes a terrifying gesture, one suggesting lewd activities, and I scoff at her craziness.

"We're just friends," I remind her, the tone of my voice reminiscent of a whiny teenager. We've been through this so many times.

"Well, that's stupid if you ask me."

"I didn't ask you. Plus, I've been burned before."

"Not by a sexy tattoo man, though. Come on. He's different."

"I don't even know him, Jodie. Besides, I didn't come here to fall in love."

"Well, dearie, I hate to break it to you, but sometimes you can't choose when you fall in love. Sometimes it just comes for you. Ask Henry. He apparently knows a thing or two about that."

I roll my eyes, laughing at the thought of Jake and Henry, at Jesse's embarrassment, and at the memory of falling into the sand laughing at his dog trying to violate mine.

Letting go of the "not a date" date with Jesse for the time being, Jodie and I stroll toward the group in the sand, the only other people insane enough to be up at this time. A few elderly ladies wearing way too tight yoga pants bend over, stretching their mats on the sand.

"Did I need a yoga mat for this?"

"No, it's fine. We can go all natural. A little sand never killed anyone, right?" Jodie says, shrugging. I feel pretty doubtful as I eye the group.

Beside the elderly ladies, a few fit twentysomethings are already warming up, contorting into crazy poses that look painful. They make it look easy.

Suddenly, I realize Jodie dragging me to beach yoga was more than just a mistake. It's going to be an epic failure, a true disaster.

"Jodie, I'm not flexible. I don't know why I let you talk me into this." Nerves creep in, and I start thinking about the million ways this will end in my utter embarrassment.

Jodie stands calmly beside me. "Because you're trying new things. Come on, it's fun. It's rejuvenating. The sound of the ocean, the feel of the sand, your body getting stronger."

"Oh trust me, it's electrifying," a wheezy voice whispers from my left.

I jump a little, not realizing someone else was listening in.

Beside me, a middle-aged man stands closer than feels comfortable. Apparently, he never learned about personal space. He, like the elderly women, is also wearing rather tight yoga pants—except his are leopard print. To go with his leopard print pants, he's picked out a black muscle tank that is leaving very little to the imagination—not that I would have really wanted to imagine his hairy chest anyway. I try not to stare at his pecs, nipples out and all, as I offer a polite grin.

I don't say anything, not really sure how to respond to a man twice my age who has just used the word "electrifying." Jodie exhales with a little snort.

"I'm George, by the way," the man says, extending his hand. I remind myself to be polite as I extend my hand to shake his.

He doesn't want a handshake though. Instead, he hunches slightly, kissing my hand as his eyes stare into mine.

I fight the urge the shake off the feel of his chapped lips on my hand and simultaneously to kick him in the crotch of his leopard print pants.

"So how old are you?" he asks, winking.

You've got to be kidding me. Yoga is not only an epic disaster. It's going to be epically disturbing.

I try not to think about the amount of sweat on his hands

or the fact he's standing way too close.

"In my twenties," I say, snapping my hand back from his grasp. This will hopefully be enough to dissuade him. God, this guy must be over twice my age. My new haircut isn't doing its job if he thinks hitting on me is a good idea—or in the realm of possibility.

"Oh, a young one at yoga. Nice. I bet you'll be all kinds of flexible."

I'm pretty sure I make an audible vomiting noise. I turn to Jodie for assistance, but she is just giggling into her hand, trying to stifle down the sound.

"Oh, George, she is all kinds of something." She winks at him, and then yanks me to the other side of the elderly ladies, beside the fit yoga attendants.

"Oh my God. Where have you brought me?" I whisper harshly, watching George like a hawk to see if he's heading our way.

"George is pretty harmless," Jodie says. "Creepy as hell, but harmless. However, I don't think I've ever seen him give such a suave kiss upon meeting someone. You are lucky, I guess."

I elbow her in the ribs as our instructor comes up to the group.

I shrug off the thought of George, although he's still making eyes at me from across the group, offering me a sad little wave as he jogs in place. I'm not sure if the waving or jogging is more ridiculous looking at this beach yoga class. Of course, the leopard print pants make everything he does seem ridiculous. Still, with class starting, I let go of the fact creepy George is still staring. Jodie comes to attention, and once I get a look at the instructor, it all makes sense now.

The early wake-up. The sand in her toes. The dealing with creepers like George.

The yoga instructor is a man, but that seems like too ordinary of a word for the being before us.

Shirtless, tanned, and toned in all the right places, the gorgeous hunk doesn't look anything like the yogi I imagined teaching the class. His crystal-blue eyes seem to sparkle as he takes inventory of his group. I turn to Jodie to see her ogling him quite obviously, a huge smile painted on her face.

"So you're purely a yoga fan, huh?" I ask, grinning.

"It's good for the mind, body, and heart," she says.

"And not too bad on the eyes, I guess, huh?" I say. Jodie just shrugs.

"I told you beach yoga was pretty worth it."

"Talk to me after class, if I haven't broken a pelvic bone."

"Don't worry, I think George will help you if you do," Jodie whispers as the instructor, whose name is Darren, instructs us to quiet down.

I make a gagging sound over the now-silent group, and everyone turns to look at me. "Sorry," I say, shrugging. "Sand in my throat."

My fit entourage shake their heads and then return their attention to Darren, making things like downward dog and warrior two look simple. I try to not fall over in the sand from my clumsiness, and from laughter as I spot George, who looks more like he's doing disco moves than yoga.

Jodie mostly just stares at Darren, fanning herself—from the warmth of the sun, of course.

An hour later, I've managed to pull a shoulder muscle, laugh out loud at one of George's poses—which led to more glares from the "fit" crew—and sweat more than if I'd gone for a jog. When I feel like I'm going to pass out on the sand, the class finally comes to a close. Thank God. I don't want to think about George rushing over to resuscitate me, and if the class hadn't ended when it did, it was looking like a very real possibility.

"Namaste," Darren mercifully says, and we chant it back. I'm thinking more like Nama-no at this point....

"Wasn't that a blast?" Jodie asks. I raise an eyebrow.

"Glad you liked class today. It's so good to see you back. It's been a while," Darren says, brushing past the ogling fit girls to talk to Jodie. I smile, give Jodie a wink, and head down to the water. I glance back every now and then to read the body language.

Oh, yeah. They're definitely into each other.

Staring at the gentle waves, I'm thinking about how much of a hard time I'll give Jodie when we get back to the apartment when I hear a voice behind me.

"You did great today, buttercup."

I squeeze my eyes shut, hoping I can zap him away with my mind.

I turn to face the music. Or George's loud pants, whichever you want to label it as.

"So, can I take you for breakfast?" he asks, grinning as he stares at me.

"Can't. Sorry. I'm working today." *And every single day for the rest of my life in order to avoid you.*

"Oh, that's too bad. Maybe next time. Have a good day," he says, winking and rushing off to catch up to the elderly ladies, perhaps hoping his breakfast date chances will work out with someone.

I turn to head back to Jodie, who is still flirting with Darren. After a few more minutes of making eyes, the two part ways, and I walk with Jodie back toward the apartment.

"Okay. You need to ask him out already."

"What? No. He's not interested in me like that."

I eye her in disbelief. "Are you serious? He's crazy about you. Ask him out. Then we can stop pretending to like beach yoga. We can avoid creepers like George, and I can sleep in again."

"I don't know. I don't think I'm his type."

I freeze in my tracks in the sand. I eye Jodie for a minute, debating what to do. Then, I think about George's creepy wink and his "maybe next time" comment.

Oh, no, George. There's not going to be a next time.

I grab Jodie's hand and yank her back toward the beach yoga area, where Darren is cleaning up his mat.

"Hi, Darren? Jodie wants to know if you would like to meet her for drinks tonight, say, eight o'clock?"

I hear Jodie inhale sharply. Darren smiles. "Yeah, I'd like that."

"Great. She'll meet you in front of Midsummer Nights. Thanks so much," I say, pulling her after me again, not giving her time to back out.

"Are you crazy? I can't believe you just did that," she hisses, but she's smiling behind her fake anger.

"Me neither. But if it means no more beach yoga, then I'm game."

"Oh, this is exciting. I need to go get my writing done so I'm ready for tonight. He's gorgeous. And flexible. And just so perfect."

"You're welcome," I say, pulling her toward our apartment, where I fully intend on heading straight back to bed.

Beach yoga checked off the bucket list. I think I'm good with taking it off completely.

Chapter Ten

"I'm going to kill you," I say through gritted teeth as I pull Jodie into the back room.

"For what?" she asks dreamily. She's still floating on cloud nine from her date with Darren last night. She got in quite late. I didn't probe her for details, but I'm thinking she and Darren may have explored their mutual flexibility.

"For that," I say, pointing to table twelve.

George is sitting, leopard print pants and red top this time. He's smiling happily, waiting for me to return with his drink.

"What's George doing here?"

"Well, you see, he says he came to see me. He heard you talking to Darren this morning at beach yoga about your work schedule and how me and you worked at 2:00 p.m. So he thought he'd stop by to see why I didn't come to yoga this morning."

Jodie covers her mouth with her hand. "So sorry. I didn't know he was listening. Darren and I were just chatting afterward."

"You know, I don't really want to be pillow talk, but some things, like my work schedule, could be discussed outside the range of creepers like George. He won't stop winking at me."

Jodie giggles a little. "Well, there's only one way to fix this."

"What?" I ask.

"You better get yourself a strong, handsome boyfriend. And fast." She winks, and I scowl, not particularly finding my stalker situation funny.

"Relax," she says, after laughing herself into tears. "I'll take over. Tell him you're busy."

"Damn straight you will."

Still laughing, Jodie heads out to the table as I sulk in the back, taking a few minutes to pull myself together.

Jodie comes back through the kitchen doors. "Hey, there's someone out there who wants to see you," she says, winking.

"Do you want me to stop liking you? Really?" I shake my head. Honestly.

"No, not George. Someone much more handsome. And he's not wearing leopard. That I know of."

I raise an eyebrow, trying to decide if she's telling the truth. I inhale, heading through the doors.

It's Jesse.

"You're a little early, aren't you?" I look at the clock. It's only 3:00 p.m. He's usually not in here at this time, especially on a Friday.

"I wanted to stop by and talk business. Hope that's okay."

"Business?" This is more confusing than the odd wave George is giving me. I shake my head and refocus my attention on Jesse. Not that it's a difficult task.

"I want to buy these," he says, pulling a few pieces of paper from a folder he's carrying. He slides them across the counter to me, and I eye the drawings with confusion. They look familiar.

They *are* familiar. They're my sketches.

"What the—" I ask, beyond confused about how Jesse got my random sketches. And more than that, I'm confused about why he's wanting to buy them.

"Jodie dropped them off with me yesterday. Said you were interested in sketching flash art for me." Jesse looks a little confused too.

"Jodie," I yell, and she turns sheepishly toward me from George's table.

"Sorry, I'm really busy over here. Unless you can pick up my tables for me," she says neutrally. George is still waving. I shrink back to the conversation with Jesse, mentally reminding myself she's my roommate so I can't stay too mad. She's on strike two for today, though.

"I just assumed you knew," Jesse says.

"Jodie must've found them in my sketchbook. Sometimes I draw in the evenings. It's just to take my mind off things."

"Well, listen, they're honestly really good. I always need new flash art."

"What's that?"

"You know, designs for when people want to look

through and pick a tattoo? These are awesome. I'd love to work something out."

"They're not that good. Besides, you're already great at designing."

"But it's always good to have a different style."

"I don't know. I'm not serious about it."

"But these say otherwise."

I sigh, looking into Jesse's eyes. He seems serious. However, I can't be sure, since Jodie basically put him up to this. I'm a little irritated she went through my stuff. I'm even more irritated she probably thought this would be a perfect matchmaking opportunity.

But I'm also a little thrilled at the idea of my art being a tattoo. I've always loved drawing and painting, though I've never felt like it was more than a side hobby. To think someone actually wants to buy my work. Boring, accountant Avery....

And it's not just any someone. It's Jesse.

"Listen, why don't you swing by the shop later. We can talk about it, work something out. Seriously, Avery. You're really good, and it seems like you like art. This could be a really fun opportunity. And if it doesn't work or you don't like it, no pressure."

"Yeah, maybe. How about if I come by after work?"

"Sounds good. Bring Henry if you want. I'd love to see the big guy again."

"Perfect. See you then."

Jesse leaves the art on the counter, smiles, and heads out the door. I stare down at the drawings, smiling stupidly at them. For a moment, I forget about the fact leopard print man is still staring at me, or that Jodie orchestrated this crazy plot.

I just think about the fact I'm excited for something, that I can't wait to get home and draw some more.

I think about how, for the first time in my life, I see possibility.

***

The shop is empty when I arrive after my shift, my drawings in hand. I lead Henry in the door. The behemoth of a dog curls up in the waiting area, practically taking over the entire space.

"Hey," Jesse says, standing at the register when I walk in. "You made it." He leans down to pet Henry on the head. Henry lets out a sigh before falling asleep.

I smile, self-consciously running a hand through my wet hair. I grabbed a quick shower after work, but was too impatient to use the blowdryer. Now, looking at Jesse, I kind of wish I had.

"Yeah. I thought about your offer. And I want to take you up on it," I say, trying to muster up a confidence I don't quite feel.

I hand over the few drawings, and he smiles. "Great. I'm so glad. Why don't you figure out a rate you want, and we'll go from there."

"Deal. I'll do some research."

"And like I said, no pressure. Just get me drawings when you feel like it."

"No pressure. I can handle that," I say, meaning it. It's good to be excited about something without feeling like it's weighing me down.

"So, what do you say we go get a bite to eat? To celebrate? I don't have any more appointments today. I'll close up early."

"I'd like that. But my hair's sort of a mess. I'm not dressed for much."

"You look fine. Trust me."

I blush at his words. "Hey, how about the sub shop we talked about? The one you said you used to go to with your dad."

"I'm offering to take you out, and you want to get some subs at a tiny shack?"

I shrug. "I'm low maintenance."

"I can handle low maintenance." Now he's smiling. "Let me just mark down some things in my books, and then we can go."

I busy myself flipping through the tattoo art book on the counter, getting a feel for what kind of drawings Jesse might want.

That's when I see it. Jesse goes behind the counter and pulls out some books. I raise an eyebrow. It can't be.

But it looks like oh yes, it can.

I surreptitiously eye the scrawled numbers, the messy figures.

"Okay, I'm not trying to be nosy. But please tell me that's not your ledger."

"My what?"

"You know, your accounting ledger?"

He eyes me with a look of confusion. "Well, yeah, I guess. I mean, it's where I track everything."

I stare at him in disbelief. "You use that thing to keep track of your records? Are you kidding?"

"Hey, I'm a tattoo guy, not a business exec. The paperwork stuff's never been my strong suit. I'll admit it."

"Well, lucky for you, it's mine. Listen, why don't you let me help you get set up with some software? It'll make your life so much easier."

"I don't want you to have to do that. You left your old job because you wanted away from it."

"No, I left my old job because I needed a change of pace. Bookkeeping for a tattoo parlor is quite a change of pace, believe me. Besides, I'm just getting you set up. I like the challenge behind it. It'll be good for both of us."

Jesse eyes the book and me hesitantly. He sighs, apparently resigning himself to the fact I'm right. "But you have to let me pay you."

"Deal. You can start by paying for my sub. I'm starving."

Jesse scrawls down a few numbers, slides his books to the side, and turns to me, shaking his head. "First, you're drawing flash art. Now, you're taking over the books. Pretty soon, I'm going to have to change the sign."

"Avery's does have quite a ring to it," I tease.

I shake Henry awake, and the dog stumbles to his feet with the speed of a slug. I yank on his collar and follow Jesse out the front door, smiling at our easy banter as he locks up. I inhale the salty breeze. It never gets old.

Jesse and I stroll down the backstreets, Henry at my side, passing wild teenagers on vacation and families trying to hold it together. We get stopped a few times to answer questions about Henry: How much he weighs, if he has a saddle, and how much he eats. A group of teen girls even take a selfie with him.

Once we maneuver through Henry's newfound fans, Jesse and I don't say a lot, just taking in the night air, the calming walk, and the peaceful company.

When we get to the sub shop, I tell Jesse to order for me since he knows what's good. He orders three cheesesteaks— one for each of us and one for Henry, of course. He knows how to get on Henry's good side. We take our cheesesteaks and fries to a tiny picnic table nearby, and I bite right in, not feeling self-conscious or dainty at all. I break up Henry's sub, placing it on the ground nearby. Henry's not feeling self-conscious either.

"It's delicious," I say through a full mouth, a piece of cheese falling to my plate. I laugh, reaching for a napkin.

"Told you. So, how many do you think?"

"What?" I ask, having no clue what he's talking about.

"How many subs will I owe you to pay you back for your services?"

I grin, wiping my face with a napkin. "Oh, I'm thinking at least fifty."

"Fifty subs for an expert accountant's advice and new art? Sounds cheap to me."

"Like I said. I'm low maintenance."

"In all seriousness, thanks for the offer. The accounting

side of the business drives me crazy. Believe it or not, I've gotten better. You should see my first-year records. Talk about a mess. You would cringe."

"Well, I'm sure it was hard getting started. What made you want to open a tattoo parlor?"

Jesse shrugs. "I was always into art, and I liked tattoos. My dad thought I had real talent. It was really the only thing I was ever good at. I worked all through high school on learning to tattoo. I pretty much taught myself, although my dad had a friend who owned a tattoo parlor back in Ohio. He sort of helped me improve my skills. When my dad died, I knew I wanted to move here in his memory. It was something he always talked about. He'd wanted to open his own mechanic business here. I'm no good at cars, so I knew I needed to come up with something else. This just seemed to fit."

"Why'd you call it J & J's?" I ask, truly intrigued.

"My dad's name was Jason. I wanted to honor him."

"That's beautiful."

"It wasn't the first year. I almost gave up. I had no clue what I was doing. I had a business loan and no customer list. I was a young kid trying to improve my tattooing, learn how to run a business, and learn how to build a reputation. It was basically a disaster. I mean, I was good at the art aspect of it. But I learned quickly that tattooing on your own and running an actual tattooing business were two very different things."

"Did you have anyone to help? How did you manage?"

"I kept in touch with my dad's friend back home. He came

up for a whole month to help me out, which was huge. But then, I was just sort of winging it. The first whole year was me having a whole string of 'oh shit' moments. Eventually, though, I found a business partner."

"What happened?"

"Things with us just didn't work out. By that point, I'd built enough of a customer base to make a real go at it."

Jesse fiddles with the napkin in front of him, taking a break from his cheesesteak. I sense some tension at the mention of this business partner, but decide not to probe further for more details. It must've been a malicious parting.

"Well, I think it's awesome. Starting a business from the ground up is no easy feat," I say, slipping the drooling Henry a bite of my sub since he's finished his own. He stares at me with gracious eyes as he swallows the bite whole, drool falling to the ground.

"Yeah. But I'm glad I did it. I'm glad I risked it," Jesse says seriously, smiling before taking another bite of his food.

"Your dad would be so proud."

"I'd like to think so. Anyway, enough about me. What about you? What are your plans for the future?"

I take a sip of my soda while I think about the question. It's a simple question—yet I have no idea what to say.

Because, in truth, I still don't quite know the answer to it.

"I'm not sure yet. I just want to explore a bit more, to figure out what actually makes me happy. I've rushed into the whole settling down thing. It didn't work out. I want to take some time and figure out what I really want, you know?"

"Are you happy?"

"I am. Midsummer Nights, Jodie, it's all helped me find a little piece of myself. And so have you." After the words slip out, I wish I could take them back. They're the truth in an odd way. Even though I barely know this tattooed business owner across from me, I feel like I do. I feel like every piece of him I uncover is a piece that makes sense, that helps me find a piece of what I want. Embarrassed to have made such an intimate confession, though, at least for the stage of our relationship so far, I avert my eyes, not wanting to be staring into those gorgeous greens as I make this confession. Yet, a big piece of me absolutely does.

He doesn't seem taken aback by my statement, though. The way he looks at me just makes me feel like he understands exactly what I'm talking about. He reaches over to pat Henry's head, the drooling dog making sad eyes at Jesse for finishing his sandwich. He says, "There's just something about being here, huh? About the waves and the sand, the people here. It just makes you feel so…"

"Free." The word is a whisper in the summer breeze. Despite the screaming two-year-old at the table behind us and the rowdy groups of teenagers passing by, the word seems punctuated in the summer air. I look back up at Jesse now, his eyes piercing right through me, underscoring the levity of the word and of the fact he gets what I'm saying.

We sit for a few moments at a grimy picnic table in front of Sammy's Subs, crinkling up our paper and laughing about a few of our recent customers. We exchange stories, share laughs, and just soak in the evening.

There's no pressure, no discomfort. There's an ease between us I've never felt with anyone else, not even Chris. It doesn't matter that my hair is air drying in the salty wind or that I have a splotch of cheesesteak grease on my tank top. Sitting here with Jesse, I feel the depth of what this place is, the depth of the freedom it's given me.

When Jesse walks Henry and me back to our place, I pause outside my door. For a flicker of an instant, I think he's going to kiss me. For a moment, I think I might want him to, despite my rules.

I know I vowed not to let myself fall again. But there's something different about Jesse, something that makes me feel like it might be okay to let go. He makes me feel like I won't lose myself. In fact, he makes me feel like I can actually find myself again.

He doesn't lean in, though, the Maryland night sky watching our amicable, platonic parting instead.

"Thanks for dinner," I say as Jesse pats Henry on the head.

"Well, I only owe you what, like forty-nine more?" He laughs.

"I think Henry is game for that. Listen, how about if I stop by tomorrow after work? That'll give me time to get a few things organized, and then I can help you get some things running."

"Sounds great. But no rush. Like I said, no pressure."

"Perfect. Thanks again."

"Anytime."

With that, we part, Henry and I going inside and shutting the door.

"Someone's falling in love," Jodie sings from the kitchen island, looking up with a smile plastered all over her face as I walk in the door.

"We went for subs, Jodie. Nothing major."

"Oh, it's major all right. And I couldn't be more thrilled. So tell me, when's the beach wedding going to be?"

I shake my head, rolling my eyes as I head into my room. "Good night, Jodie," I shout.

"Good night, lovebird. Sweet dreams."

I shut my bedroom door as Henry leaps into my bed, telling myself Jodie's just plain crazy.

But that night, my dreams are sweet… and they involve a certain green-eyed guy who may, in fact, be stealing my heart after all.

Chapter Eleven

"Hope we're not interrupting. Is everyone decent?"

I look up from the computer at J & J's to see Jodie skipping through the front door in her bright red sundress. She's got company with her—Darren, looking supersleek in his black pants and tight shirt. Jodie's grinning ear to ear, and the two are holding hands.

"Clearly we're decent," I answer, looking back to the computer as I finalize the last few steps in getting Jesse's books in order. "What are you doing here?"

"Well," Jodie says, leaning on the counter.

Jesse is standing beside me. He's been looking over my shoulder for the past hour or so, taking in all the information about accounts payable and debits and other accounting lingo.

"Darren and I are heading out to dinner and we thought the two of you might like to join us. If Jesse's done cracking the whip, that is." She winks in a creepy fashion, and I shake my head. Jesse just smirks.

"If anyone is cracking the whip, it's this one. I told her an hour ago to take a break."

"Workaholic. So boring. It's official then. You two are coming with us. Let's show them what fun really looks like." Jodie leans into Darren.

"But I'm almost done here." I really do want to finish up. I have things looking really good.

As I'm getting ready to show Jesse the next section, the screen goes black. My mouth opens, and I'm raging. Jesse pulls my hand away from the mouse.

He's turned the damn computer off. "You've done enough already. Seriously. Thank you. All the stuff you've shown me is already going to save me so much time. We can perfect the system later. Come on, I owe you. Let me take you out."

I stare into those green eyes. I want to say no. I want to finish my work. I want to say this double-date scenario isn't a good idea.

But damn, those eyes can make me do just about anything.

"Okay," I say, and Jodie literally jumps up and down clapping.

"So let's go. What are you waiting for? I'm ready to get my drink on," she says.

"Are you sure you can handle this one?" I ask, turning to Darren. He's just smiling.

"I'm not so sure. But she's worth a try."

The two now are kissing quite comfortably in the waiting room. Jesse and I pretend to stare at the floor. I finally clear my throat.

"Sorry. We just can't help ourselves," Jodie says.

"Well, try?" Jesse leads us out of the shop, shutting off the lights and locking up on the way out the door.

Darren and Jodie walk ahead of us, leaning on each other, Darren's hand on Jodie's hip. I try not to think about how awkward this is because Jesse and I are nowhere near their level of intimacy.

"So, this isn't awkward at all," Jesse says as we watch Darren's hand slip a little lower on Jodie.

"Not at all," I say, laughing.

"Do you think those two would even notice if we ran away right now?"

"Probably not for at least twenty minutes," I say, laughing. "But I can't really say anything. At least Jodie's happy. They seem to make a cute couple."

"Yeah. I guess love really is the answer for some people."

"But not for all of us."

"I'll drink to that as soon as we get to the restaurant."

We laugh now, both sharing in the common theme. I don't know what's happened to Jesse, but I sense a familiar pain and hesitancy in him. We seem to get each other when it comes to the L-word.

The four of us really do enjoy the evening. Jesse and Darren talk about tattoos and fitness. Jodie fawns over Darren. I study Jesse and try to map out more about him. After a few rounds of drinks, nothing is as awkward, even when Darren and Jodie get all googly eyed over each other throughout the night—or when Jodie rather loudly tells me she's going back to Darren's place for some fun.

When we leave, all feeling a little bit more relaxed, and Darren and Jodie go their own way, Jesse turns to me, hands in his pockets, as we walk home.

"So, what are you up to next Saturday?"

I mentally think about my schedule. "Nothing actually. I'm off work as far as I know."

"Good. I want to take you somewhere."

I feel the grin widen on my face. "Where?"

"It's a surprise."

My grin fades a little. I'm not a surprise kind of girl. "I don't like surprises."

"Correction. You typically don't like surprises. You haven't seen my kind of surprises yet."

"It makes me nervous."

"Good. Nervous means you're living right. I'll pick you up at eight in the morning."

"What should I wear?"

He thinks about it for a second. "A swimsuit."

I feel my cheeks flush. "I don't think I'm wearing *just* a swimsuit."

"So toss a T-shirt over it and some shorts. We're going to be outside, though. Consider it a beachy rite of passage."

"I don't like the sound of this."

"One more question," he says, ignoring my fears. "Are you afraid of anything?"

Now I'm really getting nervous. "Let's see. I'm afraid of spiders, snakes, clowns, and airplanes."

"Okay. Well, we should be fine then. I think."

"What do you mean 'you think'?" Now the fear is creeping in.

Jesse just laughs at my obvious terror. "It'll be great. I promise. And I'll even take you to lunch afterward."

"If we survive the surprise, that is."

"Right. If we survive."

"Jesse Pearce, has anyone told you that you really know how to make a girl nervous?"

"Avery Johannas, has anyone ever told you that you need to trust a little more?"

It's an innocent comment, but it stabs a little.

Trust.

It's something I haven't really felt for a long time. But as we say our goodbyes, Jesse looking like he might want to kiss me again but fighting it off, I smile inside.

Jesse Pearce might be a little bit wild and a little bit reserved… but there's something about him that makes me want to trust him, even if he's got me scared shitless for next week's surprise.

Chapter Twelve

"Have fun, lovebirds! Take lots of pictures. I'm so jealous," Jodie screams from the couch as I head out the door with Jesse. "Can't wait to hear where you two go."

Henry cocks his head at Jodie's animated words as I head out the door with Jesse.

"See, there's a woman who appreciates a surprise. She was practically jumping up and down when I said I had no idea where we were going."

"After today, you'll be a believer in the value of a surprise, too," Jesse says as he leads me to his car, a black convertible.

The top is down. So much for worrying about my hair looking good.

"We'll see. So can't you tell me now?"

He grins. "You really do hate surprises, huh? You'll know soon enough."

Jesse pushes his sunglasses back on his head. He's wearing simple navy board shorts and a muscle tank, showing off all the tattoos.

"I have some awesome news," Jesse says.

"What? You're going to tell me where we're going?"

He gives me a look that says "in your dreams."

"Of course not. But someone came in for a tattoo yesterday, and she picked your artwork."

"Are you serious?" The smile that spreads on my face is certainly horrifyingly cheesy, but I can't resist.

"Absolutely. She loved it. It looked great. See, I told you people would be into it."

"I can't believe it." I lean my head back against the headrest, stunned. Someone is wearing my art. Accountant Avery drew a tattoo that someone wanted to have. It's crazy. I'm thrilled.

"So now the pressure's on. You need to get more to me."

"I thought you told me no pressure."

"Well, now I have customers we need to think about." He grins, letting me know he's not 100 percent serious.

"I'll see what I can do." My head is already swirling with ideas and designs. I can't wait to get back and draw some more.

"Speaking of customers, when are you coming back for another tattoo?" Jesse asks, making conversation as we pull out of the parking lot.

The topic of discussion calms the nerves in my stomach about where we're headed. "Eventually. I want to wait until I have something I really want."

"I was starting to worry maybe you were seeing someone else."

"What?" I ask, whipping my head to look at him.

"For tattoos, I mean. I thought you had a new tattoo artist. Usually customers are back quickly, at least local customers, for a new tattoo."

I grin, inwardly chiding myself for jumping to conclusions and misinterpreting his comment. "Right. No, of course not. Besides, I've heard J & J's is on the up and up now with their financials. A girl like me respects that sort of thing." I wink at him.

"Doesn't take much, huh? Some organized ledgers, some perfect calculations."

"Stop, or I might get hot and bothered," I tease, laughing as I study the surroundings. It's a perfect, sunny day, the streets lined with people ambling toward the beach. As we stop at a red light, I laugh at a mother in a sundress yanking on her two children's hands as she screams at the father, carrying an umbrella, two lounge chairs, and at least three beach bags.

"What are you laughing at?" Jesse asks, peering over at me.

"Nothing. Just thinking you couldn't pay me to be that guy right now."

Jesse looks to see who I'm talking about, laughing as the tiny little guy saunters across the street, still being yelled at by his wife.

"It could be worse, I suppose," Jesse says. "I mean, I'm sure they'll have fun once they get there."

At that, one of the beach bags bursts, and towels, sunblock, and all sorts of things scatter onto the road. The kids are screaming, and the dad is trying to figure out what to do.

Jesse sighs, and then springs into action. He puts the convertible in park, jumps out, and helps the guy gather up the items off the street, ushering him to the sidewalk before jumping back into the car.

"That was so nice. My hero," I say once he's back.

"Don't tell anyone. I don't want people thinking the tattoo parlor owner is a softy or anything."

"My lips are sealed. On one condition," I say as the car zooms through the now-green light.

"What's that?"

"Tell me where we're going."

He shakes his head, grinning. "You'll know in about three minutes. We're almost there."

I sigh, glancing over at Jesse, whose eyes are now on the road.

How did I get here? A year ago, Chris and I were probably grocery shopping, and, if things were really adventurous, going to lunch at a local deli. Now, here I am, wearing a swimsuit in a convertible, my newly wild hair blowing in every direction, with a tattoo artist named Jesse Pearce who is surprising me with some mystery adventure.

It's funny how different life is. It's funny how I'm sitting in this convertible with Jesse, who is pretty much a stranger to me in many ways, yet I feel more comfortable than I did sitting with Chris—despite the nervousness of the surprise status.

Looking at the tattooed hunk in the driver seat, I realize with unsettling certainty that I'm okay with him being in charge. Because even though I don't know him all that well, even though we're still getting to know each other, and even though we're just friends, I can't help but think he's so much different than the love I used to know. He's compassionate and adventurous. He's supportive. He pushes me to be who I am but also to be something new.

It's weird how it took coming to Ocean City and getting a tattoo to find someone who is so good for me.

It's weird to think how, despite all my promises to myself, the sight of his rippling muscles as he grasps the steering wheel, the intricate tattoos on his arms, and the stubble on his jaw make something both familiar and foreign flutter within me.

Soon, however, I can't distinguish the fluttering of my growing feelings for Jesse from the anxious, half-vomit feelings from where the car is parked.

"No way," I say, looking up at the sign, shaking my head violently as I wonder how far I'd have to run to get back home.

"Yes, way," Jesse says, shutting off the convertible as he smiles, looking at the sign with a different sort of anxiousness.

I look back at the sign, thinking how right now, the grocery shopping and lunch might be an okay idea.

***

"Welcome to Pete's Parasailing. I'm Pete. Thanks for choosing us today. Who's ready to get up in the sky?"

My hands are shaking, and I'm still considering bolting out the door. I don't know how Jesse convinced me to even walk into this place.

This is absurd. This is ludicrous. Avery Johannas doesn't do things like this. She just doesn't, even when she's trying to reinvent herself.

"It's going to be great. Seriously. It's beautiful up there. Just try it," Jesse says to me, probably sensing my hesitancy. It's not like I'm keeping it a secret—I'm shaking like a leaf and shaking my head over and over.

"Oh, come on. Don't be scared. I'm an expert. Plus, between you and me, if I had those hunky arms to hold on to up there, I'd be all in," Pete says, pretending to whisper to me. He leans over to slap his knees, chuckling like he's just told the most outlandishly humorous joke we could ever hear.

Pete's wearing neon yellow board shorts and a Mickey Mouse T-shirt. He's got some black Crocs on and is also wearing what looks like a safari hat.

Pete, in short, looks like he's spent a few too many hours in the sun... or a few too many hours drinking margaritas. Judging by his knee slapping, I'm guessing it might be a mixture of both.

Basically, Pete looks like the last person on earth I'd trust with my life.

"Now come on, sexy lovebirds. Let's get the release forms signed and get you on up there while there's still daylight," he says, winded from his laughing spasm.

I look at the clock. It's ten in the morning.

Perhaps Pete has had too much to drink to realize it.

As he wanders to the back room of the tiny shop, I tug on Jesse's arm. "Are you sure this is safe? I mean, does he know what he's doing?"

"He's great. Seriously. He just loves his job. You'll be fine."

"I don't know. I mean, this is nice and all…."

"Hey. You said you wanted to try new things, right? Come on. You'll love it."

I take a deep breath, trying to calm my fears.

Deep down, below the raging fear and the sweaty palms, I know Jesse's right. I know this is what I came here for. I came here to be someone new, to find joy in adventure, and to live my life in a way that's exciting.

What the hell is more exciting than flying in the sky, right?

And, despite the fact Pete has questionable fashion sense, I suppose he is right about one thing.

If I'm going to be clinging to someone's arm hoping to survive, I guess clinging to Jesse's firm bicep isn't the worst thing that could be happening.

***

"You ready?" Jesse asks once we're buckled in. Despite the heat, I'm pretty sure I'm as pale as a sheet of paper, the clamminess of my skin noticeable.

"Hell no," I say. "Remind me again why we're doing this?"

"Because it's the best way to see Ocean City."

"Right. And also to die."

"It'll be fine. You'll love it, I promise." He reaches over to squeeze my hand and, for a cool second, I forget about my sweaty pits and pounding heart. I think about how damn good his hand feels in mine. It's a strong, scratchy hand—a man's hand. I think about what those hands would feel like....

And before I can finish my thought, Pete's yelling, "Here we go," over the sound of the waves and the motor. The boat lurches forward, and I let out a scream that could vie with the best horror film scream you've ever heard.

My stomach drops as we go up, up, up. I kick my feet, marveling at how quickly we leave the water behind.

Once we settle into our spot in the sky, Jesse turns to me, a huge grin on his face. "Isn't it great?" he bellows.

My gaze dances around us, glancing at the sky, at the water, and at the beach. From up here, you really can see everything in a different light. Gone is the hustle and bustle of the crazy beach life. The roar of the engine, the slapping of the water seems a million miles away. It's background music to a peaceful track of our existence up here. The rush of it is simultaneously and paradoxically calming and energizing. It's a feeling I've never experienced before.

The only way I can describe it is sheer contentment.

I nod, a huge smile now floating across my face too. I kick my feet some more, as if I'm on a swing from my childhood, enjoying the feel of the wind and the rhythmic, flapping sound of the parachute.

We don't talk for the next hour or so, just pointing at different sights as we drift around in the sky. Some dolphins crest the waves, and I giggle in delight. I'm absorbed, entranced by the sensation of being so far off the water. I'm enthralled by the view, by the adrenaline, and by the man at my side.

Before we're done, Pete dips us in the water a few times. I scream again at the shock of the waves on my backside and pray to God I don't somehow lose my swimsuit bottoms. Flying high behind the boat naked might put a damper on this whole adventure, for me and for some of the beachgoers.

Once we're back down and Pete is laughing as if he were the one in the sky, giving us a thumbs-up—I'm certain there's more than soda in that cup of his—we get situated and get back to shore.

It's so odd being back on the ground, but it's a little different too. I feel like, as cheesy as it sounds, I got a new perspective up there—of the beach, of adventure, and of Jesse.

Once we're ready to leave Pete to his own alcohol-induced devices, I turn to Jesse. "Mind if we walk on the sand a little before we go home?"

He grins. "Look at this. You're turning into a real beach girl. Can't get enough of the water, huh?"

I shrug.

In many ways, though, he's right. I'm turning into a real beach girl. I'm turning into a new person bit by bit. I'm turning into the Avery who goes parasailing and who spends the afternoon on the hot sand with a hunky man who knows exactly how to bring adventure into my life.

I'm turning into the woman I never could be before.

So when we get to the water's edge, the sun beating down on our bare skin, I'm not thinking about how I should be getting home and accomplishing something productive today. I'm not thinking about how I'm on what could definitely be labeled a date even though I've sworn off men. I'm not thinking about how I can feel my skin building up a fierce sunburn thanks to my lack of sunscreen. I'm not thinking about the pain the sunburn is going to cause in the shower, and I'm not thinking about the pain of what my next move could lead to.

Instead, I'm just feeling. For once in my life, I'm feeling instead of thinking. I'm feeling the sheer joy of doing something new. I'm feeling the racing heart and sweaty palms that aren't from the adrenaline or from the hot temperatures. I'm feeling the familiar fluttering of possibility. I'm feeling convinced that maybe love isn't all bad.

I'm feeling that at this moment, standing by the ocean waves, my hand on Jesse's arm, I want nothing more than to have those manly hands moving gently in my hair. I want nothing more than to see those green eyes looking into mine with a sense of longing.

I want nothing more than to feel those lips moving on mine, the possibility leading to action.

So I do something this new beach girl named Avery isn't afraid to do.

I turn to Jesse, the crashing waves beside us. On my tiptoes, I lean up, staring into his eyes with a confidence born of change. As he stares back at me, leaning down to meet me, I revel in the thought of letting go of the past, of the promises I made to myself, and the fear.

When my lips meet his, I surrender, only the sound of the rolling waves reminding me that we're still standing on the ground.

Chapter Thirteen

When Jesse drops me off at home, I wait until his car pulls away before dancing down the sidewalk. I jiggle the key in the lock, feeling like I'm still floating beneath the parachute.

Giving in to my heart wasn't as hard as I thought it would be. Maybe I'm just ready to let go. Maybe it's just because Jesse makes it feel easy, makes it feel real. Or maybe it's just that I'm so damn attracted to him I can't help myself.

I fling the door back, ready to finally admit to Jodie she was right. I'm in a good enough mood to deal with her "I told you sos" and her need for details.

But when I walk into the apartment, a very different Jodie greets me. My face falls, knowing my serendipitous, earth-shatteringly wonderful afternoon is going to be forever changed by the piteous look on Jodie's face and the wallowing sadness in the atmosphere.

Lysander and Reed are here too, sitting on the sofa with a sobbing shell of my roommate. Henry sleeps stretched out on their feet, lips flapping as he snores.

"What's wrong?" I ask, immediately fearing the worst.

Reed rises from the sofa to greet me, and Jodie peeks up at me through tears.

"I'm being a moron. It's fine," Jodie says as she swipes at the moisture dripping down her cheeks.

I turn to Reed, hoping for some explanation because she's clearly not fine. Nothing looks fine. He walks me to the kitchen area, where Sebastian is playing with a rogue M&M on the floor.

"Lysander and I were out last night and we saw Darren. With another woman."

My heart sinks as I turn to stare back into the living room, as if I need confirmation. I fall onto the stool at the island.

The shock sets in. We were just with Darren and Jodie last weekend. He was crazy about her. They were getting more serious by the second. Jodie finally felt like she'd found the one. She's been talking about the big, scary L-word, a word Jodie doesn't toss around lightly.

So how the hell did this happen?

I don't need to ask, however, because unfortunately, I'm all too familiar with the workings of infidelity. There isn't always a rational explanation. There isn't a flashing sign.

There's just the heartbreak of broken trust, the questions of why, and the feelings of "how couldn't I have known."

It doesn't matter that Jodie wasn't as far into a relationship with Darren as I was with Chris. *It doesn't matter.* Because the betrayal, the hurt, and the shock are the same. And the feelings don't fade with time.

Suddenly, the kiss with Jesse, the magical afternoon fades. All I see, all I feel, is the stabbing heartache I know Jodie's feeling. It's like her pain transports me back to the scene, to the heartbreak. I see him with her. I experience the sinking feeling of stupidity and shock.

Tears well in my own eyes, and now I feel like a moron for drowning in a sorrow that should no longer be mine.

"I'm sorry, sweetie. I know this probably just brings back bad memories," Reed says, putting an arm around me. I shrug him off. This isn't about me. It shouldn't be about me.

I traipse across the room toward Jodie. I sink down in the seat beside her, wrapping an arm around her and leaning into her.

"I'm sorry, sweetie. I had no idea."

"I'm a fucking idiot. I shouldn't be crying over that douchebag." Jodie wipes at her tears again, the hard, sarcastic exterior trying to return. But no matter how strong Jodie is, I know this is killing her. She thought he was the one.

"You're not an idiot. He's a fucking idiot," I say.

"I just… I thought he loved me. I thought he was it for me," she says, and the tears flow again. "I should've known."

"Hey, you couldn't have known. We all thought he was crazy about you. He fooled us all," Lysander chimes in from the other side of Jodie.

"Well, apparently he wasn't as crazy about me as that Cynthia bitch."

"Cynthia? Her name is Cynthia?" I ask.

"Yeah. She works at… um… an adult entertainment lounge down the street," Lysander adds.

I cringe. This can't help things.

"Listen, Jodie. He's a moron. But I know that doesn't help. At all. It sucks and it hurts. It's going to take some time. But you're going to be okay. You'll move on and someday, you'll be happy he showed you his true colors when he did."

She turns to look at me, a frown on her face. "I'm sorry. I'm so sorry. I'm here being all dramatic about some guy I've only been dating for a little while. It's ridiculous, especially after what you went through."

"Hey, stop. I know better than anyone that it doesn't matter how long it's been or that it's not your fault. I know exactly what you're feeling. So don't apologize. You have nothing to apologize for. We're here for you, and we're going to get through this."

"That's right, we are," Reed says. "Lysander and I have this covered. Tonight will be the sulking in your pajamas, eating ice cream night. We'll pop in a good movie and spend the night being a little weepy over this Darren dude."

"And then tomorrow night," Lysander picks up. "Tomorrow night it's ditch the dickhead night. As in, screw him, forget him, we're going out. We'll get you so liquored up, you'll be wondering who the hell Darren even is and wondering how quickly you can move on." He smiles, winking.

"Oh, I do love a good liquored-up night," Reed replies,

clapping a little. "We're good at this."

Jodie stands up now. "Really? I think you two are awful at this. Pretty sure you shouldn't put a timeline on loss. And pretty sure a psychiatrist wouldn't recommend liquored up as a technique for overcoming grief."

"Well, then the psychiatrists don't know what they're missing. Come on. Trust us. When have we let you down before? Remember the whole Aaron debacle? We got you through that, right? We've got this. Now, you two stay put. We're going to go get us all the biggest, highest calorie sundaes we can find on the boardwalk." Reed and Lysander practically dash out the door to carry out their mission, leaving us in the aftermath of their plan.

"Those two are lunatics," Jodie says, smiling. "But I love them."

I stand up now, too, leaning in to hug her. "All jokes aside, I know this isn't easy. I know it's going to take more than a few days. But those two are right. Someday you'll be happy to move on."

I pull back from the hug, and Jodie raises an eyebrow. "Does this mean you hopped into bed with Jesse? Because for a woman who has supposedly sworn off love, you're awfully adamant about this whole moving on thing."

I feel myself blush. "No, we didn't sleep together."

"You kissed then."

I want to deny it. It doesn't feel like the right time. But the uncontrollable smile on my face gives it away.

Jodie squeals, the pre-Darren-cheating-scandal Jodie showing her face. "I knew it. Oh my God, give me all the glorious details. Lots of tongue I hope? Did he cop a feel? Let's go."

"Jesus, Jodie, what are we, seventeen-year-olds?" I say, rolling my eyes to fit the persona.

But then I settle myself into the sofa and give her all the illustrious details—as if I'm a seventeen-year-old confessing about a first kiss.

For a moment, we're not two scorned lovers, two cheated-on women who feel like fools. We're just two women animatedly talking about lips and hands, and thinking about how even though love is a risk, sometimes it pays off.

***

I awake to the doorbell dinging the next morning. Rubbing the sleep from my eyes and tossing on a sweatshirt, I stumble toward the door. Jodie's door is shut. We were up pretty late last night, movies and sundaes helping keep her mind somewhat off Darren. I scuttle toward the door, not wanting the doorbell to wake her up.

I pull open the door and see quite an appealing sight. Jesse—with coffee from my favorite spot.

"Hey," I whisper. "Jodie's sleeping. Let me put on something more substantial and maybe we can go for a stroll?"

"Sure."

I let him inside where he stands at the door, coffees in hand. Sebastian, meowing wildly, runs over to rub Jesse's leg. Henry, of course, is still asleep in bed.

I dash back up the hallway to the bathroom, rushing through a hurried morning routine. I manage to slap on a few dabs of powder to take away the shine. The rest will have to do.

I slip into my room, toss on a bra and some real clothes, and head back to Jesse. He's right where I left him, Sebastian still rubbing his leg.

We wordlessly slip out the door into the misty morning, the sun barely breaking through the clouds.

"Thank you," I say as he hands me a coffee. We turn left, heading toward the sand as I sip the delicious dark roast.

"Welcome," he says. "How was your night?"

"Not so good," I admit. "Darren cheated on Jodie."

"What? Are you serious?"

"Yeah. Apparently Lysander and Reed caught him. She's a train wreck. Never saw it coming."

"Me neither. He seemed crazy about her. That was just last weekend he couldn't keep his hands off her. Wow."

"Yeah, well, that doesn't always mean anything," I say, taking another sip as my sleepy mind wanders that dark and lonely road.

We cross the street, ambling toward the sound of the waves.

"Is there anything I can do?" Jesse asks.

I shrug. "Not really. These things just take time. I know Jodie will be okay. She's strong and fierce. We're all going out tonight, though. Lysander and Reed's idea. Want to come?"

"Sure, I'm game. I'll even buy the first round," he says. I turn to him with an appreciative smile, knowing Jodie's going to need all the help she can get—from us and the liquor.

We plunk our toes into the sand, sauntering toward the water. The water that just yesterday I kissed Jesse by. The waves, the gentle breeze takes me back. Was that really just a day ago? It feels like so much has happened. It feels like the assuredness I felt in planting my lips on his has faded away, Jodie's tears and regrets taking me back to a place I didn't want to go.

I know Jesse's not Darren, and he's not Chris. But Jodie's heartache has reminded me of why the promise I made to myself was so important to me.

I've been down the road of love, and I've lost. I've been in Jodie's shoes, thinking forever was within reach, only to find out it was never even on the table at all.

Am I ready to put it all on the line again?

"You're quiet. Are you okay?" Jesse asks. We're at the water now, the chilling quality stunning me as it slaps against my toes. The bite in the morning August air suggests that summer is closing shop and soon fall will take its place. I can't help but mourn the change a little bit, feeling like there isn't just a chill in the air.

"I'm okay. The whole thing just brought up some rough feelings."

"Yeah? Of your ex?"

"Yeah."

"Want to talk about it?" he asks gently. I turn to look at him. I can tell he senses my hesitancy. I can tell he was hoping to take a walk with the woman he kissed yesterday, to revel in the bliss of our connection. Instead, he's found a disheveled version of the go-get-it woman from less than twenty-four hours ago.

I kick a little bit of water up before turning and heading a few feet back. I sit down in the sand, not caring that my ass will be covered. I twist the cup of coffee into a mound to secure it, and stare at the water. Jesse walks over and takes a seat beside me, copying my position.

"It's just.... I'm sorry about yesterday. About the kiss. I shouldn't have let that happen." Even I can hear the regretful tinge to my voice and the sadness that drips from every word. I hate that we're having this conversation. I hate that what we shared yesterday has been tainted by reality. Perhaps even more than that, I despise that I let myself get into this position at all.

A moment of silence. I can't gauge him or what he's thinking. I continue the monologue I know I need to get out.

"Jesse, I like you. I can't deny it. But I didn't come here for a new relationship. The truth is, I've been there and done that. I was in love for six years with a man I thought I'd be with forever. I gave him my heart. I never thought he'd betray me. But he did. And so when I came here, I swore I wouldn't let it happen again."

Tears are now trickling.

"It's okay. I understand. I get it, I do. I haven't had a great time with love either. It's a risk. Such a risk." He exhales, the words sounding like a chore. Still, I can see on his somber face that he understands where I'm coming from.

"It is. I just don't want to get consumed again."

"But that's the thing, Avery," he says. The sound of my

name from his lips jolts me out of my tears. I turn, the sun peeking through the clouds a little more as we stare at each other. "I'm already consumed."

My heart slams into my chest, a suffocating but also energizing feeling pulsing through my veins. These are confessional words I didn't expect to hear. These are words that certainly contradict my "no love" vow. However, as scared as I am, as adamant about not falling in love as I thought I was, the feeling in my chest tells me one more thing—whether I want to admit it or not, my heart craved these words from Jesse.

As I try to acclimate to the words he's just spoken, Jesse continues his own monologue, one very different than I'd expected. "Look, I've had my share of shitty relationships. I've seen that love doesn't always work out. First, I saw it with my mom burning my dad like she did. And then I had a relationship I thought would last forever. It turned out to be a disaster too. I told myself I wouldn't let myself get roped into a relationship again. I told myself I didn't need love. And then you walked into my shop."

"Jesse, I—"

He interrupts me. "Let me finish. You walked into my shop, and I was consumed by you. Not just physically, but just everything about you. From that first time sitting at Midsummer Nights to our walk on the beach to our kiss, I knew there was something different about you. I know it hasn't been long, and I know I shouldn't fall this hard so fast. I'm still scared, Avery. But that kiss yesterday, well, it made me think maybe it's okay to be a little scared. It made me feel like it's worth it. You're worth the risk."

I want to argue. I want to get up and run away. I want to resist those green eyes, that soft look.

But when Jesse's lips find mine this time, I let him take the lead. It's a strong kiss filled with all our floating emotions—lust, passion, and most of all, fear. We're two dilapidated people with two scarred hearts. The pain of our collective pasts might be too much for one couple to handle. We might drown or at least be swept far from the safe shores we're used to.

His hand finds my hair, and I melt, right into the sand beneath me.

I'm still scared as hell. I'm scared because it's too soon to let my heart find love again. I know I should let it breathe. I'm scared that I'll get hurt. I'm scared that, just like last time, things will seem perfect and then they'll end with my heart being chopped by the axe of unfaithfulness, of betrayal.

But, as the kiss sends a jolt right through me, warming me in all the right ways, I'm also scared of saying "no" to this feeling. I'm scared of letting him go over fear of what might not happen.

So, for the second time, I let Jesse Pearce's kiss ignite me, the conflagration building between our hearts hot enough to scorch the sand beneath us.

The kiss burns.

Chapter Fourteen

"But you know I like purple."

"Purple's too innocent. Red says, 'Come and get me.' Red says, 'I'm forgetting him.' Trust me."

Reed and Jodie are arguing in the living room over her shirt. She's already had Alexander do her hair and makeup—Lysander had him do a house call since this is quite the emergency, in his words. She looks stunning, a bold smoky eye screaming from her face. Now they've just got to work on the outfit.

"Avery, tell her. Doesn't the red one look better?" Reed asks. I'm standing in my doorway, a skintight black dress clinging to me. This was also a Reed find. He insisted that a night out with Jesse Pearce meant I needed to look a little badass. Thus, he's added a studded bracelet and some gladiator sandals. I feel a bit punk and a bit silly, but Alexander, Reed, and Lysander assured me I look like sex walking.

Whatever "sex walking" means or looks like. Besides,

it's not like I'm ready for sex with anyone tonight.

"I do like the red, Jodie. But I think you should wear what you want. This is your night."

"Yeah, some night. The sad, single Jodie needs an entourage to escort her out so she doesn't repulse men into other women's arms."

"Stop it right now," Lysander said. "He's trash. Worse than trash. He's a flea climbing on the trash. Now just trust us. We're going to help you have fun. You'll see. It's better without that boring yogi man. Tree pose? Please. So overrated. We need to find you someone who can actually show you a good time."

"If you say so," Jodie says, looking to me now for help. I just shrug.

"So where is that sexy hunk of yours, Avery?" Reed asks me as Jodie heads to her room to change her shirt.

"He should be here any minute."

"I think it's so great you're moving on in the love life department. See, we told you that you just needed a new haircut," he says, winking at Alexander.

"What can I say? I'm just a regular little matchmaker. No one can resist my hairstyles."

The doorbell rings. "I'll get it," Reed says. "I need to eye up Avery's man candy, make sure he coordinates with her."

"I'm wearing black. What's there to coordinate?"

"How do you women manage? I swear. You girls should just hire me to be your stylist. Honestly." He rushes to the door. I shake my head. I seriously don't know how you couldn't coordinate with black.

Jesse's at the door. He's wearing tight black jeans, a black muscle shirt, and a royal blue button-up. He's also wearing sneakers. He looks sophisticated somehow despite his unsophisticated combination.

"Perfect," Reed says, appraising his outfit. "You two are going to look so hot together."

I get ready to jump in and save Jesse, a little embarrassed that Reed is appraising his outfit. But Jesse honestly doesn't seem to mind.

I step away from the doorway of my room and saunter closer to him.

Jesse doesn't take his eyes off me. It's like that Cinderella moment every woman dreams of, the one where the sexy guy seems to only notice you.

I've rarely had that moment. I had it on my wedding day and once during my honeymoon. But that Cinderella moment, that look, faded with time. I didn't think I'd ever see it again.

Standing before Jesse, my heart pounds. I'm getting that moment again.

"You look gorgeous," he says, a whisper escaping his lips. I notice Reed and Lysander whispering in the kitchen, but I don't turn to look.

All I look at is Jesse, the man I get to be with tonight.

As we get ready to head to the limo Reed rented for us—he said if you're going to party, you need to do it right—I lean into Jesse.

"You're right. It's worth the risk."

He kisses my neck, and I feel the melting feeling again.

"Damn right it is."

"Get in, lovebirds. We have some partying to do," Lysander says, ushering us into the limo as Alexander passes around champagne.

Jodie's already downing a glass as we get in. "Well, Alexander, looks like you and me are the fifth and sixth wheels. You sure you're gay?"

"Totally sure."

"Damn." She downs another swallow of her champagne as the limo pulls out, taking us out for a night that's sure to go down in the books.

***

"Dance with me?" Jesse asks as I toss back another shot.

"I'm not a great dancer."

"And you think I am?" He grins. "Let's do another shot, and we'll both feel like dancing queens."

"Another shot? Sounds fabulous," Jodie proclaims. She's already had quite a few. I'm pretty sure Darren is nowhere near her mind, judging by the way she's hanging on the arm of some tall and tanned guy. I smile. Maybe Reed and Lysander do know what they're doing.

We order another round and then head to the dance floor, my head spinning just a little. I've passed on a few rounds, vowing not to wake up with a hangover tomorrow.

I've also vowed not to let things get out of hand. The more time I spend with Jesse, the more likely it becomes. No matter how hard I want to fight these feelings, no matter how much I tell myself not to get hurt, I can't resist him. Those eyes, that smile.

But more than that, it's who I am when I'm with him. It's the fact I can be the rational, math-loving Avery. I can be the Avery who plans out her outfits for the week and who has exactly one sugar packet in my iced tea, no exceptions. I can be the somewhat-of-a-worrier Avery. He likes me for who I am.

With him, I'm still the same Avery—just better. He makes me want to let go a little, to live a little more. He makes me believe maybe I can pursue this whole art thing, even on the side. He makes me want to try fried pickles and to say to hell with fear, flying in the clouds. With him, I want to be me but braver. With him, I have more fun. With him, I feel like I'm exactly who I'm supposed to be.

So as we dance on the floor, the pumping music making me shake my hips a little sassier, his hands wandering a little lower, I relax into us. I relax into the idea of Jesse, of starting over with love, of opening my heart again. I give in to the idea that this could work.

"I'm falling for you," I whisper into his ear, a sultry confidence partially emblazoned by the booze in my bloodstream and partially by the revelation that I'm willing to let him in.

He pulls back, those green eyes piercing mine with such an intent stare. "I'm falling for you, too."

Our lips meet, and I succumb to the electricity between us, the dancing couples around us fading away. It's just Jesse and me, two wandering souls brought together, the sweaty atmosphere only heightening the pulsating in my veins.

Things can't get any better. I feel a soul-defining

verification that this is exactly how things are supposed to be. With his hands on my waist, I feel like maybe this is how life was supposed to go, like all the pain it took to get to this point may just have been worth it.

But before I can float away in a rosy bubble of bliss, my perfect moment is popped by the sound of a sultry voice that isn't my own.

"Jesse? Oh my God, is that you?" the voice says. I turn to my right to see the girl it belongs to.

It's a busty blonde who looks like she stepped right off the catwalk.

And with the sight of her, with her approach, my confidence starts to fizzle. I take a step back, as if to physically recognize what my heart is seeing.

Love is never easy, and no matter how much verification you have that it's for real, there's always something strutting in the way.

***

Jesse stands for a long moment as if he's not sure what to do. He looks at me and then at the model of a woman before us. "Kat? What are you doing here?"

"Came back in town for the weekend. It's so good to see you," she says, leaning in to touch his arm. They're yelling over the music, and it feels like I'm in some horrific teen movie from the 90s. I stand gracelessly, appraising the situation, trying to read body language and gauge who she was to him, or who she is to him.

Fear creeps back in, taking icy hold of my veins, of my lungs.

But before panic can set in, before the things I felt seeing Chris and Nora come back full swing, Jesse speaks up, his voice lacking the warm quality I've come to love. "Well, have a good night," he says, grabbing my hand and pulling me toward the bar. His words are frigid, and his movements scream he's uncomfortable. I follow, but not before turning to eye the woman who just interrupted our moment.

Kat stands in the middle of the dance floor, hand on her tattooed hip, which is visible since she's wearing a crop top. It's a heart—simple, sleek, and vulnerable.

"Can we step outside?" Jesse asks me, whispering in my ear. He looks flustered, and I'm terrified as to why. Is this going to be where it all ends? Is this going to be my reality check, the moment that defines my life as "forever alone?" Just when I thought I could open my heart up again, it's cracked in pieces once more. I don't think I can do this.

I put on my brave face, however, and nod. Jodie's sitting and giggling wildly at a table full of sexy men, and Lysander and Reed are kissing in a corner nearby. They're too drunk and having too much fun to notice my mini crisis. I'm on my own.

Hand in hand, we stroll out of the club and amble toward the sand, the water's rustling not calming me in any way. Jesse leads me to a bench and pulls me down. I sit, uncomfortable in what's about to happen and in the knowledge that this could be where it all ends.

"I'm sorry. I know I'm acting strange. I just had to get out of there."

"So I'm guessing Kat and you were a couple?" I ask

gently, trying to mask the fear in my voice.

"Yeah. Years ago. She was my business partner at J & J's."

"Oh, really?"

He nods, looking at me. "I'm sorry, Avery. Please understand. It's just—she was a huge part of my life for a while. Things were serious."

I nod. I can appreciate that. I think about how I'd feel seeing Chris tonight. You can move on from the past, but you can't forget completely. When your heart feels emotions as strong as love, it's not like you can just erase that.

"You loved her."

"I did. For a long time."

I try to tell myself it's okay, that this doesn't mean anything. I tell myself not to cry. But deep down, the disappointment is creeping in. The realization that love is a minefield settles into my heart, and suddenly the sultry glances and the electrifying kisses start to fade away.

I look into Jesse's green eyes and I still see the potential for love. But I also see pain, the pain that will be mine if this doesn't work out.

Because, I'm starting to believe again, love never really works out.

Jesse sighs. "I'm sorry. I don't want to ruin our night over this. Honestly, it's in the past. It's just… she really burnt me. And when I see her, it just brings up feelings of such anger. I don't want to be mad anymore. I want to move on past it. But when I see her and remember what she did, I just get this anger in my chest."

"What happened?"

He looks down at his feet. "Things were going well with us, but as I told you, the business was struggling a little at first. Running a business is stressful and hard. Kat decided she wanted a different lifestyle. She didn't want to be counting every dollar hoping for a miracle. She wanted a bigger life than I could give her, and she wasn't willing to wait and see how long it would take for that to happen. So, one day, she picked up and left. She took half the money, took half my stuff, and checked out of our life together. She just left me a note that said she needed a change and she was sorry."

I reach for his arm now as he clenches his jaw. Behind his anger, I see something he isn't saying.

I see the pain of rejection. I see the little boy who wondered why his mom up and left. I see the slap in the face it must have been when Kat repeated his past.

I see the fear that isn't so different from the fear in my heart.

"I'm sorry."

"Yeah, well, I should've been used to it. I saw what my dad went through. I don't know why I thought it would be different."

We sit now, lost in our individual memories and regrets. We sit, two adults scorned by love and by people we trusted. We sit, two broken people unsure and unsteady of where we should go next.

"Jesse, look. I meant what I said. I'm falling for you. But maybe we're not ready. Maybe we should slow down.

I'm scared."

He pulls me up from the bench, putting a finger to my lips and then kissing my cheek. "I'm scared too. I'm scared shitless, if I'm being honest. I'm scared to love you. I'm scared this won't work out and I'll be lost again. But you know what I'm more scared of?"

I just look at him.

"Letting you go. Letting the past get in the way of this. I don't want our pasts to be the line in the sand between us. It's scary as hell giving in to this feeling. But I think it's scary to let this go," he says, pulling me into him. "I'm sorry I got distracted. Please know, though, she's the past. You're my present."

I smile, the tension floating away. "The present," I reaffirm. He's right. This is scary as hell. But with his arms around me, I feel more at home for the first time in a long time. I feel like maybe scary is survivable.

"When I was little, I was terrified of the water," he says as we kick off our shoes and toss them on the bench before heading down to the water's edge. The tide is high, and the waves plummet into one another, the sound echoing in the night. "The first time we came to the beach, I cried when my dad tried to get me into the waves."

"Some beach boy," I say, grinning, as we get closer to the edge.

"You know what my dad did?" he says.

"What?"

"He threw me in. He tossed me in, just like that."

We're at the water's edge now, the darkness only

interrupted by some streetlights on the sidewalk way behind us, and the full moon. It's a little eerie out here now, the stars and the moon our only company. It's calming, too, in an odd way.

We stand for a moment, the water lapping against our toes.

"Will you jump in with me?" he asks, turning now, holding both hands out.

I breathe in the salty night air, thinking about the question. It's dark, and it's scary. The water is probably going to get rough along the way, and it's shockingly cold.

It might drown me.

Yet, holding his hand, I can't believe Jesse Pearce would let me drown. It might be wishful thinking or even naivety, but I think Jesse Pearce might be the one to jump in with.

Instead of answering him, I lean in, kissing him as the waves violently thrash behind us, reminding us of the danger of being out here. As we kiss under the stars, the memories of Kat, of Chris, of our pasts fade into the breeze as we let it all go, crossing the line in the sand for real this time.

Chapter Fifteen

"Is this too much?" I ask Jodie, pointing to the sundress I'm wearing with gladiator sandals.

"Are you kidding me? You look perfect. Va-va-voom! Look at those boobs in that dress," she says, giving me a thumbs-up from her spot on the couch.

I shake my head. "I'm not going for va-va-voom. It's not like that yet."

"So you're still delusional. Good to know. And people call *me* crazy," she says, slamming her laptop shut. "Don't you have garlic bread in the oven?"

"Shit," I exclaim, dashing toward the oven, praying I'm not too late. I swing open the oven door, a blast of heat slapping against my face. I exhale, relieved to see perfectly brown garlic bread. Another minute, and things would have been on the decline.

I grab a faded pink pot holder and pull the tray out, awkwardly trying to figure out where to put the hot cookie sheet. The stove top is filled with boiling spaghetti, sauce, and meatballs.

"Here you go," Jodie says, crossing the room to come to my rescue. She puts down a hot plate, one that looks homemade, and I toss the pan on it. "How long until hot stuff is here?"

"Five minutes."

"That's my cue."

"You don't have to leave."

She gives me a look. The typical Jodie look. "Oh, I'm leaving. I don't want to be here if some action takes place. I'll pass. I'm weird, but not that weird."

"I feel bad."

"Why? I'll just head down to the Coffee Shack. I do some of my best writing there anyway."

"You sure?"

"Yes. And I'll make sure I come home extra late. And I'll knock twice."

I roll my eyes as I turn off the burner for the spaghetti pot. "No need. Nothing will be happening."

"Well that's a damn shame."

She leans down to pat Henry on the head. Henry has plopped himself in the middle of the kitchen, right where he's the ultimate tripping hazard. I step over him like I'm stepping over a log to get to the sink.

Jodie saunters to her room to change as I finish preparing dinner. I've set two plates at the island and two wine glasses. It would be fancy—if we didn't have plastic forks and paper napkins to go with it. Oh well. I'll just work with what I have.

There's a knock at the door.

"I'll let him in. I'm just leaving," Jodie sings, dashing from the hallway before I can even think about getting to the door. Nervous tension rises in my chest.

You're being ridiculous, I tell myself. This is just dinner. It's not a big deal.

But I think the butterflies in my stomach are more aware of what's happening than my brain—because I've felt them only one time before.

My mind almost travels back to that tiny bistro where I met Chris, but I don't have time, mercifully. My naively nostalgic thoughts are interrupted by the swinging open of the door, the sight of Jesse, the sound of Jake running toward Henry, and Jodie screaming, "She's all yours. And I mean *all* yours."

I feel my face burning, so I busy myself with carrying the pot of spaghetti from the sink back to the stove.

"Dinner's almost ready," I say as Jesse steps in and Jodie shuts the door.

"Jake, no," Jesse screams, just in time for me to turn with the pot of steaming spaghetti sauce in my hands. Jake is beelining for Henry—and he's got that familiar, frisky look in his eye.

It is at this exact moment, as I'm straddling Henry on the way back to the stove, that Henry, perhaps afraid of Jake's motives, decides to stand at attention.

It is also at this moment that I and the pot of spaghetti sauce go flailing across the tiny kitchen like a bad 80s romantic comedy.

***

When I was little, my mother always insisted I "sit like a lady" in my sundress at church on Sundays.

Legs sprawled, my sundress flipped upward toward my face and my Victoria Secret hot-pink underwear showing, I'm not quite sure this is what she had in mind.

I lie for a moment, staring at the ceiling, trying to pretend this isn't happening. There is currently sauce everywhere. I even see a splatter on the ceiling. I'm in such a state of shock, I haven't yet decided if the boiling sauce has landed on me and melted off my skin. Glancing at my arms, I don't see any burns or red splotches, so I think I've managed to avoid scorching myself.

"Are you okay?" Jesse asks, kneeling at my side beside a puddle of spaghetti.

"I think so," I whisper, yanking down my dress. When I put these underwear on today—which match my bra—I was definitely not planning on Jesse seeing them. But, if he did happen to see the outrageously expensive underwear and bra I bought, I didn't plan on it being like this, legs sprawled after an awkward near-death experience with boiling sauce, two dogs lapping up the remnants of our dinner in the kitchen.

Tears well. What a freaking disaster everything is.

Jesse collects the now-empty pot from near my head. On a positive note, I didn't give myself a concussion with the Rachel Ray cookware, so that's a plus.

"So, I'm guessing it might be a little while until dinner?" he asks.

I exhale, but in spite of the ludicrous situation, a smile creeps onto my face.

And then, before any tears can fall, I laugh. Like, ridiculous, snorting laughter. I turn on my side, holding my stomach as I laugh so hard I think I might hyperventilate. It's contagious, because pretty soon, Jesse is laughing too.

Eventually, we try to shoo Jake and Henry away before they eat so much sauce they go into diabetic shock.

"I kind of want to let them go," Jesse admits. "I mean, the more they eat, the less we have to clean."

I sit up, blowing a strand of hair out of my eyes. I take inventory of the disaster.

Despite Henry and Jake's best efforts, there is sauce everywhere.

I mean everywhere.

"I'm sorry. This is a disaster." I sigh again, shaking my head. Maybe I should've stuck to the whole swearing off romance idea because judging by this, I don't think I'm winning any awards in that department anytime soon.

Jesse smiles. "It's fine. I mean, I love cleaning up spaghetti sauce off every inch of a kitchen. It's a good challenge."

I shake my head. "So I guess I'll get cleaning."

"I'll help."

I glance around. "God, what a mess. Where do we even start?"

Jesse bites his lip, looking around as Henry and Jake continue lapping up sauce. "I have no idea." We both shake our heads, laughing, because what else can you do?

As we gather the strength to pick ourselves up and Jesse reaches for paper towels, I head for the mop and bucket.

We each pick an end, sopping up sauce from every inch of the kitchen. I sort of wish now I hadn't made a double batch. If I didn't have such a sexy cleanup partner, I'd probably be scowling and using quite a few expletives.

Jesse doesn't seem to mind our miserable job, though. In fact, he's whistling while he scrubs up the specks of sauce.

When we're nearing the end of the monumental task, which includes scrubbing Henry's and Jake's saucy paws, I turn to Jesse. "So what are we going to do for dinner now?"

I don't have time to make new sauce. So far, we've got spaghetti noodles that are waterlogged because I haven't been able to strain them, and garlic bread.

Jesse eyes me. "Chinese?"

"You read my mind," I say as I finish mopping the final corner. "Sounds heavenly." I reach for my phone and hit speed dial for the Chinese restaurant around the block.

As the phone rings, I realize I have no idea what Jesse wants. "Oh, what do you want? What do you like?"

"Surprise me," he says, tying the trash bag to take outside. "I'm a man who likes surprises."

He heads outside with the trash bag, Henry and Jake following him to the door. I call in an order, picking what I suspect Jesse will like. Once he comes back inside, I grab the bottle of wine from the fridge and pour us each a generous glass.

"God, that was a disaster," I say, smiling. "To messy beginnings." I hold my glass up to clink with his.

"To messy beginnings."

"I guess it could always be worse," I say, feeling a twinge of optimism.

"Absolutely. It wasn't all bad," he says, before taking a sip of his wine. For a moment I want to ask what he means by that.

But then I think of the pink underwear and the somewhat indecent display.

That can't possibly be what he means, can it?

Get a hold of yourself, Avery. Slow down.

But if we're taking it slow, why do I keep getting all flustered, all tingly, when I think about Jesse seeing me on that floor? Why do I keep wishing, just a little, that he'd helped me peel off that dress? Why am I having an odd kitchen floor fantasy—minus the sauce and such?

I need to get it together, or this could be a whole lot more dangerous that a spilled dinner. The va-va-voom Jodie mentioned could be a premonition for something even more indecent than the scene in the kitchen.

As I head to the door to greet Chuck, the local Chinese restaurant delivery boy, I start to wonder if maybe it *is* a good thing that Jodie's going to knock twice.

***

When I come back into the kitchen and set the bag on the island, I take in the sparkling sight. Thankfully, there's not a trace of sauce anywhere. The only reminder that my first dinner for Jesse was an epic fail are the take-out Chinese boxes he's getting out of the bag.

At least I've uncovered one thing, though.

The man can clean.

Check off on my list of qualities I love in a man. Although I've sworn to myself I wouldn't be checking off any this summer, and if I were, I'm pretty sure some of the physical attributes would rank higher than this anyway. Mad dusting skills or mad bedroom skills? I'll choose the latter. Hey, I might be rational and a little square, but I'm no saint.

"I'm so sorry for ruining our night. I didn't plan on cleaning and eating takeout when I invited you over."

"Pretty sure you didn't ruin it. Although Jake and Henry seemed to enjoy your pasta sauce and I'm sure it was delicious, Chinese food speaks to me." He digs right in. "Yeah, you got it. Sesame chicken. My favorite."

His grin is so huge I decide not to dampen it with the truth—the sesame chicken is my favorite. I actually bought him General Tso's.

But I guess that's the thing about us. We don't know all the details about each other yet.

It's weird starting over. As much as I don't want to think about Chris, it's so odd having to learn all the little things about someone again. It's unsettling to have to uncover all the nooks and crannies of who Jesse is. With Chris, I knew his favorite food at every restaurant. I knew that he didn't like apple juice, and that Adidas socks were his favorite. I knew he couldn't stand the smell of nail polish remover, and that he loved watching the news on Monday mornings to get his week going.

The truth is, as I plop the food onto my plate, there's so much I don't know about Jesse.

Then again, as I turn in time to see him making Jake and Henry sit for a piece of chicken, there's so much time to find it all out. It's scary, but it's also exciting. Looking at him as he smiles at our dogs, I realize I don't see it as work to get to know him. I see it as an adventure. I want to get to know him, every inch of him, on every level.

"So, tell me about you. Tell me something I don't know," I say, deciding it might as well be now that I start uncovering some pieces.

"Like what? I'm an open book," he says, grinning.

"Yeah, okay. If you say so."

"Well, what do you want to know?"

"Um, well, when you're not tattooing or eating at Midsummer or walking Jake, what do you do? What's your hobby?"

"Napping. I'm a fan of naps." He fiddles with the chopsticks that came in the bag as I opt for my fork. He chases a piece of chicken around his plate, and I shake my head at his answer and at his choice of utensils. He finally nabs the chicken and shoves it in his mouth.

I offer a mock clap at his skills, and he pretends to take a bow before switching to his fork. "Wow, impressive," I offer.

"The naps or the chopsticks?" he asks.

I shake my head. "Clearly both."

"I also like video games, if that helps."

I raise an eyebrow, and Jesse playfully shrugs. "What? Don't tell me you hate gamers. Please don't tell me that."

"I didn't say I hate them. I just don't get it. I mean, why

waste so much time when you could be doing something productive?"

"Because the point of a hobby is to do what you like, not be productive. And let's give me some credit, here. It's not like I've got bloodshot eyes and am missing work because I've logged five hundred hours on *Skyrim* or anything."

"What's *Skyrim*?"

Now his jaw drops. "Are you serious?"

"Yeah. Not much of a gamer, I know that's shocking."

"All right, that's it. I'm adding to your bucket list. You're going to play *Skyrim*."

I shake my head. "No, I'm good."

"Come on. Have you ever played a video game?"

I tap my chin. "Nope. Never."

"Why not?"

"Just didn't have time."

He shakes his head. "Well, we're going to change that. You and me. Tomorrow night at my place. I'm going to open you up to the magic of *Skyrim*."

"Really?"

"Really. How's seven o'clock?"

"Fine, I suppose. But on one condition. Are you going to feed me?"

"Yes. I'll prepare my favorite meal. On one condition."

"What's that?"

"You can't blame me when you get addicted."

"I'm not really worried about it," I say, laughing as I gobble up some more food.

Looking across the table at him, his silent, stoic maturity

mixing with this new, childlike side, I grin. There are so many layers to him, so many walls to tear down. He already seems so different from the tattoo parlor owner I met that first day. It's a good thing.

Together, it seems like we're coming out of our shells, stepping away from the past and the hurts that haunt us. Together, it feels like we can just be ourselves, whatever that means.

I want Jesse Pearce to win over my heart even more than he has. I want to believe we can do this. Maybe we can fight the odds and win at love despite all our prior obstacles.

Settling onto the stool at the island, talking about the upcoming fall craft festivals at the beach and Jesse's hopes for expansion, I can't help but think maybe we can, a little spilled sauce and all.

It might not be perfect, but I'm starting to realize perfect isn't what I need—just in time for me to accidentally spit a piece of rice across the table as Jesse tells me about the latest video he saw on *Tosh.0*.

Chapter Sixteen

"Dammit! I hate this," I scream, a piece of cheese flying from my mouth. "How do I complete this task?"

Jesse laughs, taking the controller from me and tossing it onto the sofa. I startle, looking at him as if to say, "What the hell are you doing?"

"Come on. Maybe we should take a break. You can beat that mission another day." Jesse laughs, picking up another slice of pizza from the box. Henry is drooling on his leg, and Jake is sitting at my feet panting. Both have had way too much pizza, but both just want more.

After last night's pasta debacle, as I'm calling it, Jesse decided to play it safe and serve his favorite dish—which happens to be D.J.'s pizza right around the block. I'm not complaining. At least there won't be any sauce disasters.

"I kind of want to finish though."

"I've created a gaming monster," Jesse says, talking in what seems to be a Frankenstein voice. It's more cheesy than realistic.

"We haven't even been playing it that long."

"Three hours."

"What?" I scream, jumping from the couch. I look at the video game on the screen, the gorgeous colors of the fantasy world jumping out at me. "You let me play this thing for three hours?"

"Not like I had much of a choice. You weren't really taking your eyes off the screen."

I cover my mouth with my hand, chuckling. "I guess you were right, this thing is a little addictive. I'm sorry. You're probably bored."

Jesse stands now, shoving the pizza further back on the coffee table. "Nah. I liked watching you. Your technique is quite interesting, especially when you pull the good ol' button mash."

I laughed. "That thing is fun. I sort of get it now."

"Good. But I am a little worried you're going to turn into a closet addict. Start missing work, stop taking calls."

"I would never." I don't say this with much assurance.

I yawn, wondering what to do. Should I go? Should I stay? I want to stay, but this whole dating thing has too many damn unspoken rules. What am I supposed to do?

"Hey, this place has a small balcony off my bedroom. Want to do some stargazing?" Jesse takes the reins for me. Although the word "bedroom" sends a chill up my spine. Lord, maybe Jodie's right—maybe's it's been way too long.

The thought of staying a little longer, though, entices me. "Sure."

"I'll grab some beer. Follow me," he says, and I obey,

traipsing across the fluffy carpet of his living room to the tiny galley kitchen.

He leads me through his bedroom. It's what one would expect from a masculine bachelor pad.

Barren.

There are no cute quote pillows on the bed or anything on the walls. I guess Kat's claws weren't in very deep, or Jesse did a good job at obliterating any female presence in the apartment. It looks utilitarian and efficient, nothing more. There aren't too many socks piled on the floor by the hamper, and the bed is sort of made, so I guess Jesse earns points for being more organized than me.

Not that it matters. Not like I'm moving in or anything.

"Sorry. The place could use some decorating, I know," Jesse says, as if he's read my mind.

"No, it's…."

"Boring? Plain? Not sure what adjective you were going to fill in the blank with."

"Efficient?" I ask, as he slides open the glass door that leads to a tiny balcony. From here, there's a nice view of the backstreets of the city. The humid air blows my hair as I take the beer he's handed to me and lean over the edge just a little. It's the warmest night we've had in a while, so it feels good to get a blast from the hot summer air.

"Not sure efficient is what you want in the bedroom," Jesse says, and I smack his shoulder. "Well, am I right?"

"I'm not answering that," I say, feeling myself blush. The buzz of the alcohol we've been drinking, though, is numbing me a little bit. "This is really cool."

I look down to what would be the front of J & J's tattoo parlor.

"Whoa, easy," Jesse says, pulling me back.

"I'm fine," I say, grinning. "It's not like I'm going to fall."

"I'm not taking any chances. I don't need any cracked skulls in front of my place of business."

"Might draw attention," I tease. We quiet, staring out at the starry sky. This isn't exactly primo stargazing property. The streetlights blot out a lot of the good constellations. Still, I can pick out a few from my astronomy class.

"Do you come out here a lot?" I ask, still staring at the sky.

"Yeah. It's nice after a long day of work to just wander up the stairs and head straight out here. It's a good place to think."

"It's peaceful."

"When there isn't a tattoo machine buzzing below, yeah."

"Do you want to eventually move out? Get a house or something?" I ask.

"Yeah, we'll see. With just me and Jake, it works, you know? It's easy for me to go to work and to come check on him. But someday, if I have a family, I don't think living above the tattoo shop will always work."

I nod, looking further out into the distance. A family. He used the word "if," but that means it's a possibility.

I guess he hasn't completely closed all the doors, either.

We stand for an hour or so, talking about all sorts of topics.

The thing with Jesse is we never run out of things to talk about. He comes off as shy and quiet initially, but the man can tell stories that go on for days.

I involuntarily shudder, the night air picking up and chilling my bare shoulders. This blast of warmth isn't fooling anyone—fall is lurking around the corner. I can feel it.

"Do you want to go back in? You look cold," Jesse says. I nod. But then I freeze in place as he gestures toward the sliding door. I tentatively step toward the door, sliding it open.

Another awkward dating dilemma. Do I linger in the bedroom, my thoughts obvious? Or do I run straight out of there, beeline for the sofa in the living room, to safe territory? Option A would obviously scream that I'm moving fast and a bit horny. Option B would scream I'm not interested at all and am verging on asexual.

Neither are prime options. Although, if I'm being honest, the problem is I haven't quite decided which camp I'm in. Obviously, my body is rooting for the sex-it-up option. Jesse's damn hot, he's got charm and personality, and I'm falling for him more and more. The buzz of the alcohol only adds to the appeal of the first choice.

However, the reserved side of me says it hasn't been that long, that I need to go slow. Even in an alcohol-induced haze, I can still sense the danger of going all in.

Decisions, decisions.

"So, can you stay for a while? Maybe we could pop on Netflix?"

Again, Jesse's taken over the driver's seat. I exhale in relief. "Yeah, that would be great."

I walk casually toward the living room, pretending I'm not inwardly imagining him grabbing my arm and tossing me on the bed, thrusting the covers away and thrusting in all sorts of other ways, too.

Thank God he's not really a mind reader, or I'd be uncovered in more ways than one.

***

There's an eerie light coming in my window. It's not at the right angle. Did I move my bed or something?

When my eye slowly cracks open, I notice something else weird. There isn't a purple wall or even a yellow wall from the living room.

There's a white wall, an unrecognizable flat screen in front of me.

And my head isn't on a pillow.

It's on a lap.

I jump, startled by the foggy realization.

"Jesse," I screech, shaking him. He's leaning at an odd angle on his neck, the navy plaid of the couch his only support.

"Ow," he says, rubbing his neck right away. "What the—"

"I think we fell asleep. What time is it?" I scramble from the couch as if I'm a teenager who's been out past curfew. I grab my cell phone from the coffee table. It's eight fifteen in the morning.

We slept through the night.

"Jesus, it's eight fifteen."

"Do you have work?" Jesse asks, still working out the kink in his neck.

"Shit, yes. I'm on at eight thirty." I scramble to find Henry, who after some thorough investigation of Jesse's apartment, is on his bed. Slobbering. Jake is on the bed, too, sidled up against Henry.

Go figure. My dog spends the night in Jesse's bed while I fall asleep lamely on his sofa.

I notice Jesse's pillow is sopping wet with drool. Great. As if this can't get any better.

"I'm sorry," I say, turning to Jesse who is now behind me observing the same thing.

"It's fine. Could be worse. Anyway, just leave Henry here. He's comfortable. I'll let him and Jake out later. You can stop and get him sometime tonight."

Tonight. Another night with Jesse. This is becoming a regular thing. But I think I'm okay with that. More than okay with that.

"Maybe tonight we won't fall asleep like grandparents on the couch. Wow, we're bad at being wild and fun."

Jesse laughs, still rubbing his neck. "Yeah we are. Oh well, I guess we just got comfortable. Although I don't know how the hell we did that, judging by my neck. Jesus. Maybe next time we should watch Netflix in bed."

I startle for the second time this morning.

"Shit. That sounded like a total come-on," Jesse says, rubbing sleep from his eyes.

"Was it?" I ask, my morning sleepiness perhaps dulling

my censor.

"Maybe. But listen, you'll have to think about it all day at work and decide. You're going to be late. Get out of here, woman."

"Gladly. See you later. Thanks for a good night."

"I'm not complaining because I did have fun. But this is sort of the strangest date night I've ever had. I mean, between the falling asleep on the couch and waking up fully clothed to the huge dog you're leaving drooling in my bed, I'm not sure what to make of it."

I shrug. "Guess you'll have all day to think about it. Thanks for watching Henry. Hope he's not too much trouble."

"I'm sure Jake won't mind," Jesse says. I lean in to kiss his cheek goodbye, trying to forget about the morning breath I most definitely have.

Jesse doesn't seem to notice the breath because he leans right in, claiming a kiss from my lips, lingering for a moment. I'm almost tempted to call in sick and spend the day exploring those lips a little more.

The old Avery still very much inside, I snap back to reality and decide to be responsible. I dash out the door and hightail it toward Midsummer, thinking about how weird it is I'm doing the walk of shame into work—but I didn't even have sex.

***

"Uh-oh. Walk of shame, folks," Jodie announces as I scuttle through the door of Midsummer Nights. Luckily, it's an hour before opening, so it's only Lysander and Jodie.

I've made it with only a minute to spare.

"What are you doing here?" I ask Jodie as I rush behind the counter.

"Why, hello to you too, dear roommate. Why yes, I'm feeling great this morning."

"I didn't mean it like that. I just mean you don't usually work this early."

"I'm filling in for Joseph. He called in sick." Jodie's already getting place settings ready for the morning crowd.

"Big surprise, huh?"

"Enough of this small talk. Give me the details."

I shake my head, trying to simultaneously smooth out a wrinkle on my sundress. Pretty sure I'm not looking too professional this morning.

I head to the coffee area behind the counter and pour myself a cup.

"You look rough. Although, your hair isn't too messy. Sex hair is supposed to be messier." Jodie leans on the counter across from me, fluttering her eyelashes as if she's waiting for the scoop.

"I think to have sex hair you have to have sex," I mutter between sips.

"Are you kidding me? You were gone all night with Mr. Hot Stuff, and there was no sex? What, did you guys spend the evening knitting blankets?"

"Playing video games and watching Netflix."

"Oh my God, you're reprehensible. Both of you. What, are you both a hundred? You do know that at an adult sleepover, you're not actually supposed to sleep, right?"

"We had a good night."

Jodie smirks, shooting me a glance. "I'm starting to wonder if you know what a good night means. Jesus. Just get on with it already," she teases, heading to the kitchen area to start prepping some things for the first customers.

I smile, shaking my head. Lysander is at the bar area, where he's been listening in.

"You know, she's kind of right. I see the way you two look at each other. What are you waiting for? You're two consenting adults who are single. I can tell you're crazy about each other. What's the holdup?"

I busy my hands with a cleaning rag, wiping off the counter that's already spotless. "I don't know. I think it's just a big step, you know?"

"But don't you think you're ready?"

"I don't know. I'm falling for him. Hell, I might even be *in* love with him. But to start another relationship seems so risky."

"Honey, I don't think you have a choice. I think it's already started. So why half-ass it?"

"That's right," Jodie says, giving my bottom a little slap. I jump. "Get your whole ass in the game." She slaps my ass with a towel, making an over-the-top whipping sound effect as she does.

I give Jodie a playful shove before speaking up. "You're ridiculous. That Craigslist ad made you seem so sweet."

"Well, didn't your mother ever teach you not to believe everything online?"

"Yeah. She was worried you were a serial killer. She had

no idea it was even worse."

Jodie lets out a creepy, maniacal laugh, and Lysander laughs from across the room. Despite her nosiness and her constant tendency to dissect my sex life—or nonexistent sex life for now—I'm glad to see her laughing and happy.

It might even be contagious, because despite the fact George stops by for some breakfast and stays through the lunch hour, I can't seem to wipe the smile off my face. Despite my wrinkled outfit and smudged mascara, I feel refreshed and hopeful, even if I did mess up the whole adult sleepover thing.

Chapter Seventeen

"Oh my Lord, will you two just sleep together already? I can't stand your googly eyes for each other."

It's Tuesday night, and I'm on break—in Jesse's booth, of course. We're holding hands across the table, only pulling away to eat a fried pickle every now and then. Jodie is leaning on our table, rolling her eyes at us but grinning.

"You know, you pushed for this. This is kind of your fault," I say, my mouth full.

"I know. Don't remind me. I'm great at matching everyone up but myself," she says, turning to see Reed sitting at the bar area, laughing with Lysander. "It's just a freaking Valentine's Day commercial in here."

"What about that Martin guy you met over the weekend?"

"Yeah, well, without the tequila clouding my judgement, I realized he's a little nasally."

"Shallow much?" I tease.

"Not all of us just stroll into a great relationship."

"You'll find the one. Give it time."

"In the meantime, I'll just gawk at you two and live vicariously through your romance."

"Fried pickles. Such a romance," Jesse jokes.

"It's romantic to me." I pretend to swoon.

"Okay," Jodie announces, standing up. "I draw the line at talking about Jesse's pickle. That's where I'm out."

I feel myself blush, and Jesse just shakes his head.

"So honestly, just sleep with each other, get it over with. God, this tension is noticeable across the room. Lysander," she yells to the bar. "Can you let Avery off early? She needs to go get laid."

"Jodie," I shriek. "Customers are listening."

"Honey, you're not fooling anyone. They all know I'm right."

An elderly couple in the booth near us looks appalled. I look long enough to notice, however, that the woman eventually shrugs, and nods as if in agreement.

It's mortifying.

I want to climb under the table, but Jesse just squeezes my hand to comfort me. How the hell did I go from swearing off men to having my sexual desires discussed in a restaurant?

Life has taken quite the turn.

Jodie rushes back to her table.

"So, anyway," Jesse says, grinning. "Before you get back to work, I wanted to show you something."

"Boy, am I glad you waited until Jodie left to say that." I grin.

"Here," he says, pulling a folded-up paper from his wallet. "What do you think?"

Before me is a picture from what looks like a home interior magazine. In the picture is a bright blue wall with a mural in the middle. The mural is made to look like the wall has been torn away, almost like paper. In the middle is an underwater scene, gorgeous in its execution.

"First, I'm wondering when you find time to read *Home & Garden* magazine."

He shrugs. "A guy has his secret pleasures, right?"

"Pleasure. Now that's a nice word," Jodie says as she walks by to give the elderly couple their drinks. I jump and shake my head.

"Anyway, I was thinking this would look nice at J & J's. You know, sophisticate it up a little bit."

"Yeah, I think it looks neat. Not too classy."

"So you don't think J & J's is classy?" He raises an eyebrow.

"Well, I didn't mean it that way."

"I think you did."

"I didn't, really."

He sighs, putting a hand to his chest. "You know, I work really hard to make J & J's come off as sophisticated, and to think one of my artists doesn't think it is. Well, that stings. There's only one way I think you can make up for it."

"What?" I ask, a little confused about where he's going with this.

"Let me hire you to paint this."

I shake my head. This was *not* where I thought he was going. Apparently I've been around Jodie too long. I need to get my head out of the gutter. My cheeks heat.

"Why are you so red?" he asks.

"Nothing… it's just…. Never mind."

His grin widens, and he raises an eyebrow. "You thought I was going to ask you something indecent, didn't you? My, my, Ms. Johannas. Get your mind out of the gutter."

"I did not," I vehemently reply, although it's an utter lie.

"Anyway, what do you say? Will you do it? I will pay you… with money, just to be clear." He winks now, and I can't help but giggle before turning serious.

"I don't think I can do it. I'm not good enough."

"You know, I hear you always doubting yourself, but your work says otherwise. You tell me you can't draw, and then I have your flash art flying out of my book onto people's skin. You tell me you can't possibly go parasailing, and then you do it and love it. You tell me you're not that good at painting, but I've seen your work. Have some faith. You've got it."

I look at the picture and then at Jesse. He believes in me. I should say no, that it will be too risky and too much work. What if I can't do it?

Then again, what if I can? The thought of painting, of doing something creative, appeals to me.

So, after a long moment, I nod. "Okay. When can I start?"

"Whenever you have time. No rush. You can come paint whenever you want. I already cleared off the wall."

"Mighty confident I would say yes."

"Come on. How could you resist my charm? Especially over fried pickles?"

I smile. "What if it looks horrible? What if it's bad for business?"

"It won't be. It will be fabulous. And besides, if it's terrible, we can always hang a few posters over it. No worries."

I raise an eyebrow. "Such faith you have."

He grows serious for a moment. "I do have faith in you. I just wish you had faith in yourself."

I nod. "Well, I better get back to work before Jodie comes back over and makes some sexual innuendos."

"Okay. I'll see you later then?"

"Okay. I'll swing by after work so we can get things started."

Jodie passes by and winks at me.

"Don't even say it," I command. She puts her hands in the air.

"I wasn't thinking anything at all." She chuckles to herself as she heads to the bar for the next drink order.

Chapter Eighteen

"Whatcha sketching over there?" Jodie asks from her seat on the sofa, her feet tucked underneath her. I'm on the recliner, rocking my sweatpants and my favorite hoodie.

"Sketching some new tattoo ideas."

"Can I see?"

I shrug, passing the book over.

"Oh my God, Avery, these are so good. Jesse really snatched you up at the right time. Holy hell, girl, you are an *artist*."

"I'm not really that good."

"Not what I heard. I had some customers last night talking about the mural you're painting at J & J's."

"No, you didn't." I shake my head. It's just a mural.

"Right hand up to God. I had a table of cute guys talking about the hot blonde who was painting a totally awesome mural, in their words."

"It's seriously not that good."

"Will you give yourself some credit? You're good. Own it."

I smile. If only it were that easy.

I've been working hard on the mural painting at Jesse's tattoo shop. Every day I get off from Midsummer Nights or sometimes even before I go in, I drop by with my painting clothes and get to work. At first, I was nervous as hell, but now I've fallen into a groove. And although I don't think I'm quite the rave-worthy artist Jodie seems to think I am, I have to admit it is looking pretty good.

Pretty good, though. Not truly praiseworthy level.

Still, with every stroke of the brush or of my pencil in the sketchbook, I get closer to the truth: I love this. I love the feeling of the creativity flowing through my veins and out for the world to see. I love the satisfaction I get when my work makes someone smile or say, "I'll take that tattoo." I love the feeling of not being constrained by a box or by a spreadsheet of figures.

I love the freedom of my mind. I wonder what life would've been like if I'd been pursuing this all along.

I remind myself not to get so far ahead of myself. This is just a hobby right now. There's a big difference between being a hobby artist and being a "real" artist. The self-doubt creeps in at the mere thought.

"Anyway, I'm glad you're doing something you enjoy."

"Me too," I admit. "Now get back to work. You're on a deadline, aren't you?"

"Yes. I keep telling my agent you can't rush the creative mind, but apparently he needs to eat or something. The artist's life isn't easy, I'll tell you that."

I smile, taking my sketchbook back to continue working

on the bird I'm sketching.

***

The mural takes me ten days. Once I start working on it, I literally can't stop. I become a bit obsessed. Jesse often has to bring in takeout just to remind me to eat.

When it's finished, though, I'm damn proud of it. It's better than I imagined, and I'm sort of in shock that I did it. I painted it by myself.

Maybe this whole art thing could work out, at least on the side. Staring at the realistic ocean painting, I take the brush and sign my initials in the bottom corner.

"How's it feel to be a famous artist?" Jesse says, sneaking up behind me and planting a kiss on my cheek.

"I wouldn't know."

"Well, you're going to soon. This is awesome. Really. You're amazing."

I turn in his arms, the paintbrush still in one hand. "Oh yeah?"

"Yeah." He takes my lips in his, and all the thoughts, doubts, and even successes melt away. I'm just the woman in Jesse Pearce's arms—and I'm okay with that.

Because I know in his arms, I'm really not *just* a woman. I'm Avery Johannas, the woman who eats fried pickles and goes parasailing. I'm the woman who is finding her way through waitressing and painting. I'm the woman who draws tattoos and is damn proud of it. I'm the woman who goes out on Fridays to the club and who no longer gets her nails done regularly, because the ocean water just erodes them anyway.

In Jesse's arms, I'm the woman I never knew I wanted to be. Even though it took me a while to see it, loving Jesse was exactly what I needed to truly be free.

"So, let's celebrate tonight. Go home. There's a surprise for you there. Meet me back here in about two hours."

"You know I don't like surprises."

He raises an eyebrow.

"Okay, they're growing on me a bit."

"That's my girl. Now get moving. I have work to do."

I steal one more kiss before putting the paintbrush down on the drop cloth, taking one last look at my masterpiece, and scurrying home to find whatever Jesse has waiting for me.

***

I can't help but wonder if the pink dress is supposed to be a reminder of the pink underwear incident. Nonetheless, the strapless dress Jesse's left for me fits like a glove. I feel damn good in it, which isn't something I would usually say.

I toss on some ballet flats with it and put on the pink Sabika necklace Jesse has also left for me. No man, not even Chris, has ever given me this romantic movie moment.

Jodie's at work, so I don't get to hear her wolf whistle or innuendos on my way out the door. I'll admit, her lewd comments are growing on me. I actually feel a little lost without them.

Still, this is just a thank-you for the mural. This isn't going to lead to sex—necessarily.

But on the way to Jesse's place, my palms are a little sweaty and I feel a little fluttery in my chest. I feel like a sixteen-year-old going over to her boyfriend's house because his parents are out of town. I feel like a woman whose life is about to change.

***

There's some soft rock music playing when I open the door to Jesse's apartment. The distinct smell of teriyaki sauce permeates the room, dancing in my nose as soon as I walk through the door.

"Hey. That looks amazing on you," he says. He's wearing black jeans and a button-up shirt. He's gelled his hair, and hints of his cologne permeate the room.

"Thanks. I love this. You didn't have to do it."

"I like to treat my artists well."

"So you do this for all of them?" I ask, setting down my bag on the counter.

"Only the good ones."

He leans in to kiss me, and I realize how natural this has become. It hasn't taken long for us to settle into couple status. In retrospect, it seems now like it was always coming. It seems unnatural for us not to be like this—comfortable, kissing, and together.

I'm so glad that for once in my life, I broke my own rules.

Jesse leads me to his kitchen table, which is adorned with a dozen pink roses. I smile, gently touching the petals of one.

"This is beautiful. Thank you."

"Have a seat. Dinner is ready." Jesse brings out a few casserole dishes with rice, teriyaki chicken and vegetables, and even some egg rolls.

"Did you make all this?" I ask coyly, pretending to be impressed.

"Yeah, it was sort of rough because I'm not that great at cooking."

He stares for a moment as he sets the dishes down. I can tell he's trying to see if I believe him.

I look directly from him to the top of the refrigerator, at a large take-out bag with a familiar Chinese restaurant's name. I raise an eyebrow.

"That's an old bag," Jesse says, waving a hand but smirking.

"Yeah, okay. I just have a feeling this is going to taste just like it."

"Only because I worked so hard to get the secret recipe."

I dig into the dishes, serving myself, laughing at the trouble he went through. "You know, you didn't have to dirty dishes on my account. I would've been fine with takeout. I'm not a food snob."

"That's a good thing, because I'm not much of a cook."

"Oh, and I am," I say, referring to the pasta debacle.

"What a pair, huh?"

I shrug. "Could be worse."

"I'll drink to that," he says, holding up his bottle of beer. We clink bottles as we finish eating. To an outsider, I'm sure it looks ridiculous. My fancy dress and necklace, sitting at a table eating take-out Chinese food.

To me, though, it's perfect. The man I've fallen for sitting beside me, Chinese food, and a comfort I haven't had with anyone else.

As much of a mystery as Jesse Pearce was a few months ago, he's become as familiar as my new self.

I like this new Avery. I like Jesse's Avery. I like the Jesse and Avery we are together.

So when we finish eating and he gives me the look I've come to recognize, I lean forward, kissing him with a fervor I've reserved for this moment, telling him wordlessly that I'm all his.

As he leads me back to the bedroom and hastily unzips the dress he painstakingly picked out for me, I smile.

For a long time, I didn't think I wanted to belong to any man. For a long time, I thought this part of myself was shut down.

But as Jesse's hands travel down to the familiar hot-pink underwear I'm wearing, I feel myself let go of all those ideas I had before.

I've come to realize it's okay to be his, because Jesse doesn't hold me back. He makes me who I want to be. He makes me the best version of myself.

Loving him might be a risk, and losing myself completely to him tonight might be my undoing. Letting him go, though, is not an option, not when he tosses me back on the bed, and I feel every part of my being succumb to the tattooed hunk moving perfectly on top of me.

And so, after a night of learning what adult sleepovers

are actually all about and mastering the sex-hair look, I let go of my rule.

I'm all in. I'm all his.

Chapter Nineteen

When my eyes open in the morning, I stretch gloriously as I stare at the bare, white walls of the now familiar room. I wipe the sleep and remnants of last night's mascara from my eyes.

There's no doubt I'm rocking sex hair this morning, I realize, as I attempt to run my fingers through my knotted, frizzy locks.

"Morning," a groggy voice whispers as lips find my neck and start kissing me. A smile comes to my face.

"Hey," I say, turning to see Jesse right next to me, his head actually on my pillow, his bare skin against mine.

Normally, I'd worry about morning breath. I'd feel like I should leap out of bed and start tackling a million to-do lists. Ordinarily, mornings lounging in bed with naked men aren't my thing.

But looking at his body as he rolls to his side and props his head up with a hand, I think maybe I could get used to this.

We look at each other for a long moment.

"Breakfast?" he finally asks, and I nod quietly.

"Shower first?" I ask. A grin spreads on his face.

"I think that's a great idea."

I follow Jesse unabashedly into his shower, stepping over a snoring Jake on the way. The shower takes a little longer than normal, and our breakfast is delayed. I try not to analyze it like I tend to do. I try not to worry about the what-ifs and the hows and the logistics.

Instead, I try to let my heart lead the way, my now patched-up heart, and think about how even though love can hurt, sometimes it can just feel so damn good.

***

Wet hair dripping down my back, I walk hand in hand with Jesse to a nearby diner for breakfast. Our conversation is as languid as our pace—we're both basking in an easiness that has opened up from giving in. Love isn't about sex, that's for sure. But sex with Jesse has made me realize just how much I wanted this and just how much I want to be with him.

As we order two humungous omelets and rounds of coffee, I check my phone for the first time.

There's a text from Jodie full of emoticons that, when paired together, seem suggestive. I smile and shake my head.

There are also two voice mails from numbers I don't recognize. A little worried something is wrong, I put the phone to my ear.

When I hear the words of the message, I look across the table at Jesse, confused and stunned.

The second voice mail is somewhat similar to the first but from a different number. I slowly, quietly exit out of my voice mail and put my phone on the table.

"What's wrong?" Jesse asks.

"I think you might have some explaining to do."

A grin spreads on Jesse's face. "Did you get some calls for painting?" His eyes light up devilishly.

"Yes. The strangest thing happened. Two random people called and said they'd got my number from my business card and want to know if they could hire me for some work. You wouldn't know anything about this business card, would you? Because last I checked, I don't have a business card."

Jesse smirks and reaches into his pocket for his wallet. He pulls a bright teal card from the front of it and slides it across the table.

I see my business card for the first time.

Avery Johannas, Artist
Specializes in murals, landscapes, and canvas painting
Call for a price quote

In the corner of the card is a lily, the same one gracing my shoulder. I am speechless and confused. I'm amazed that Jesse went through all this work for me. I'm a little embarrassed to see the word "artist" by my name, and overwhelmed at the thought people actually want to book me.

I'm also quite impressed by how good the card looks.

"Are you mad?" Jesse asks, seeming to consider the prospect for the first time.

I hesitate, looking up at him. "No. I'm just... amazed. People actually want to hire me."

"Of course they do. You're awesome. I don't know why you're so shocked. I've been having people rave about your mural all week, and it wasn't even finished. I know I may have overstepped with the business card thing, but Avery, I see how you light up when you're working. I can feel your passion for it from across the room. I also know you're not confident in your abilities. I felt like you just needed a little shove in the right direction."

I flip the card over and over between my fingers, considering his words. I think about how much I loved painting that mural, about how good it's felt to explore something that never felt like a possibility. I think about how amazing it would be to follow this dream.

But a tiny voice in my head also tells me this is ludicrous. I hear my parents' words telling me that art isn't a real career. I hear Chris's laughter when I once told him I thought it would be fun to be a painter. I hear all the "I can'ts" and all the reasons this is nuts.

Looking across the table, however, at those green eyes looking back at me with such a resounding faith, I shove the second set of thoughts aside. Across the table is a man who believes in me enough to make me a business card, who trusted me with his tattoo parlor walls.

There's a man who, despite past hurts, has trusted me with his heart.

I decide that if he believes I can do it, I can trust in his faith.

So instead of answering him, I pick my phone back up, call the bakery and the doctor's office that left messages, and book my first two jobs as an artist. Who knows where it will all go, but like my relationship with Jesse, it's time I find out.

Chapter Twenty

I've never been the woman from the movies—the one who walks seductively in her dress that clings in all the right places, her eyes screaming confidence and sexual energy. I'm usually the girl who walks like a clomping goat in high heels and who has no sense of fashion. I'm the kind of girl who can't pull off the serious photo face, and usually ends up looking constipated. I'm not glamorous, and I'm not usually sexy. I'm usually just a hot mess.

Tonight, though, things are different. In my red dress with a more scandalous slit than usual, I feel like one of the women from the movies. I walk with my head held high and what I imagine to be a sensual glimmer in my eye. As we walk into the four-star restaurant we've had reservations at for over a month, I feel like a movie star.

It's him. He does this for me. Being the woman on his arm makes me feel like I'm better than I truly am. The way his blue eyes drank in the sight of me when I emerged from our bedroom this evening wearing my new outfit made me *feel like a woman worthy of his love.*

"It's stunning," I whisper to him as we're led to our private table.

"So are you," he says, leaning in, his cologne drifting around me. I get butterflies at the scent of it. It's the same cologne he was wearing the night we met. It's the same cologne he wore on our wedding day. It's the scent that just stirs me.

Once at our table, Chris pulls out my chair. Always the gentleman, he radiates class as he marches to his own seat, cracking open the menu. I feel a little flutter in my chest when I open my own menu and start to notice some of the prices.

"This place is expensive," I whisper. Chris just grins.

"You're worth it. We're worth it. It's not every day you celebrate your fifth anniversary."

Champagne arrives soon after and we place our orders. The whole time, I feel like I'm in a dream. The whimsical lighting, the elegant music in the background, and the classy diners around us make me feel like royalty.

All of that, nonetheless, is just backdrop to him. Sitting in the restaurant, I can't take my eyes off him. His perfect jawline, the eyes that scream at me from across the room. I can't believe how lucky I am.

I can't believe that this man, the man who stole my heart at a tiny café in the middle of the city over a messed-up bagel order, is mine. I can't believe this man who is sexy and sophisticated, intelligent and brave, is looking at me the same way.

We spend the night enjoying our dinner and talking about memories. When we get home, we spend the entire evening wrapped up in each other, the sheets tangled around our sweaty bodies.

When I finally drift off in his arms, I think about how blessed I am. So many marriages fall apart, but not mine. Five years in and we're still going strong. We're still madly in love. We're still the couple who goes to fine restaurants and talks for hours. We've got the chemistry and the connection.

As I drift off to a different version of dreamland that night, I think about how fortunate I am to be able to be so confident in my forever.

***

Staring at the ceiling, Henry snoring on the bed beside me, I mindlessly shove my hair out of my face as my mind comes out of its memories. In some ways, the red dress anniversary, as I remember it, seems like yesterday.

In other ways, though, I don't even know who that woman is. Fine wine, the fancy restaurant… at the time, it seemed like a dream. In many ways, it was.

But now that memory, that dream, is tainted by the truth. That night, I thought we'd mastered marriage. I thought we were untouchable. Now, I realize how naïve I was to think an expensive dinner and a few rounds of sex could solidify forever. I feel idiotic to think I was so easily appeased and reassured.

I was a fool who thought being the woman on his arm

was the best place to be.

I groan as I sit up, exhaustion from working the late shift settling into my bones, and mental weariness from thinking about today's significance burning in my head.

August 27.

Today would have been our seven-year anniversary.

When I flipped the month on our cat calendar, the date jumped out at me like a flashing warning sign. I didn't want to see it or even acknowledge it. I tried to tell myself it didn't matter anymore.

But it does matter. It will always matter.

It's not that I miss him. It's not that I wish things had worked out differently, necessarily. There's so much about my life now that I'm thankful for, especially Jesse.

Still, the day I vowed forever to a man I wanted to spend it with is a big day—even if that forever only lasted a limited amount of time.

I just feel—shitty. Slouchy. Down.

I could go work on one of the two murals I've been hired for. I could go to the beach for the day—Jodie and Jesse are both working. I could go visit them at work or go shopping. There are a million things I could do.

But none of it seems fitting. So, after letting Henry out for his morning pee, I grab myself a cup of coffee, park myself on the couch, and drown myself in binging on *Teen Mom* and forgetting about my own dysfunctional life for a while.

***

"Uh-oh. What's wrong?" Jodie says six hours later when she bursts through the door and flings her keys on the coffee table.

I'm still huddled in the same position on the couch, Henry and Sebastian both snuggled against me. I got up once to pee and once for another cup of coffee. Other than that, I've spent the day watching drama unfold on TV.

I look up, self-consciously running a hand through my semigreasy hair. "Nothing. Just relaxing."

Jodie eyes the television, raises an eyebrow, and then grabs the remote, flicking off the show. She sits in the chair near the couch. "Spill. What's wrong? I get needing a day of relaxation, but when you start bingeing on *Teen Mom* so much that I think you're stuck in the sofa, something is wrong."

I readjust myself as if to prove to Jodie, and myself, I'm not actually stuck in the sofa. Sighing, I start fiddling with my nail polish, methodically picking at a chip in the mint green color.

"It's today. The date. It's my wedding anniversary. Or, well, it was."

Silence. No words come from Jodie. No judgements or questions. I look up, and she nods.

I feel the need to continue. "I know it shouldn't matter. It's not like I still love him, and I have this great thing with Jesse. I have a new life. But, I don't know, I guess it's just kind of a slap in the face. The fact that I really thought love could last forever. I feel like a fool. And I feel more like a fool for sitting here sulking. I just—"

Jodie puts up a hand to quiet me. "You don't have to explain. I get it. I mean, I've never been married, so I can't get it too much. But I do see where you're coming from. You thought you had forever. You didn't. And even though you know now there's a life past that broken forever, I'm sure it still hurts. It's still scary how wrong you were. And spending six years with a man and then breaking up can't be easy. I know you say you don't love him, but I think there will always be a part of you that will mourn him. How could you not?"

I smile, grateful that this amazing roommate and friend gets me.

"Now, we need a plan. We need to ditch this place and stop sulking. I am not spending the entire evening watching *Teen Mom*. Although I must admit, the show is pretty juicy."

I raise an eyebrow. "I don't picture you as the *Teen Mom* binger."

She shrugs. "We all have our secrets. Anyway, go wash that hair of yours. I'm going to get a quick snack and check in with my agent. Then, we're going out."

"Jodie, I really don't feel like clubbing."

"Relax. What, do you think I'm so one-dimensional that going out only means partying?"

I give her a look.

"Okay, fine. But listen, tonight, no partying. No men. No alcohol. Wow, on second thought, this is sounding like a bummer. Anyway, we're going out, doing the whole tourist thing. Girls' night on the boardwalk. We'll play some stupid, rigged carnival games and eat enough funnel cake to make us puke. What do you say?"

I smile. "Sounds perfect."

Energy from Jodie spreading to me, I pull myself from the sofa. Sebastian and Henry quickly fill in my space as I head to the shower, ready to rinse off the regrets, the date, and the feeling that still lingers from a love that no longer is.

***

"I can't believe you got into a fight with that guy," I say, laughing hysterically as I carry a stuffed panda in one hand and a funnel cake in the other. Jodie's hands are loaded down with two huge lemonades. We meander to the side of the boardwalk and find a bench. I set the panda between us.

"Well, the sign clearly said you got a level-two prize. He was just trying to rip us off. Hot or not, no one is ripping me off."

"And what are we going to do with this huge panda anyway?"

"Maybe Henry will like it," Jodie says as she rips into the funnel cake. She drops a piece back on the plate. "Damn, that's hot."

We sit for a moment, seagulls flocking around us hoping for a rogue piece of funnel cake to drop. The sun is fading into the horizon. We watch a few leftover beachgoers play in the surf as the salty air whips into our faces. I take a deep breath, feeling at peace.

"This was fun," I say. We'd spent the afternoon and early evening hours playing carnival games, going in silly souvenir shops, and watching a boardwalk magician. We'd giggled like two teenagers on spring break, winding through the crowds as we talked way too loud and ate way too many greasy foods.

"It was. I haven't been down here for a while. We should do this more often. Although, I feel like the carnival games would be more fun if we went drinking first."

"I think Reed and Lysander would agree with that statement, for sure. In all seriousness, though, thank you, Jodie. This was just what I needed."

She rips back into the funnel cake, deciding either it's cool enough or it's worth the risk of scalding her mouth. I follow suit, washing down a huge piece with the lemonade.

"No thank-yous. But I agree. This was what you needed. This can be our yearly tradition, what do you think?"

Looking out at the waves, I smile to myself. Yearly tradition. I have a yearly tradition here. It's hard to believe a few months ago, I wasn't sure if this would work out. Now, I can't imagine it not working out.

It's only been a few months and I'm still figuring so much out. But sitting on this bench with Jodie and a huge stuffed animal, I realize I'm home. This is where I'm meant to be.

We finish the funnel cake and talk about the latest episode of *Jane the Virgin*, our favorite show. Afterward, Jodie convinces me to go to the Ripley's Believe It Or Not! where we get lost in a mirror maze and stare at replicas of the world's marvels. When we emerge from the recesses of the boardwalk museum, it's dark out. The sky is alight with perfect stars, although they're murky because of all the neon lights on the boardwalk.

"You hungry?" Jodie asks.

"Not really. The funnel cake was a lot."

"Well, get hungry. You've got an ice-cream date," she says.

"What?"

"Yep. I'm dropping you off at the Dairy Queen on Ninth. Jesse's waiting for you."

"I thought this was girls' night," I say, confusion on my face.

"It was. But I texted Jesse to meet you there. We had our fun, but now you need a reminder of why today's date eventually won't matter. That marriage, Chris, it was all just a road bump to your real forever."

It's an uncharacteristically serious moment from Jodie. I want to argue, to say that Jesse and I aren't that serious. I want to be mad that Jodie is yet again meddling behind my back. But I'm not.

I just smile, walking toward Ninth with a lot more enthusiasm and an appreciation for a roommate who always knows just what I need.

"I love you," I say to Jodie, and she nudges me with her shoulder. She takes the panda from me.

"Love you back. Now get your ass moving. There's a hottie waiting to buy you ice cream. I'd be running."

"Why don't you come too?"

"And be a third wheel, watching you two make googly eyes at each other? I'm okay. Me and Mr. Panda here will make our way back to the apartment."

I raise an eyebrow. "You're going to get caught up on *Teen Mom,* aren't you?"

"Of course not," Jodie says, but the grin on her face gives her away. "I've got work to do."

"If you say so."

I have a suspicion that whenever I wind up back at home tonight, Jodie will have filled in the space I occupied all morning.

***

"See you later," Jodie says as we get to Dairy Queen and spot Jesse sitting on a bench. He's wearing jeans and a *Game of Thrones* T-shirt, sprawled out on the bench by himself. When he sees me, he jumps to his feet.

"Hey," I say, heading into his arms. He kisses me, and I realize this is exactly what I needed all day. With the touch of lips, any lingering feelings of sadness melt away.

"Get a room, you two," Jodie yells from a few feet up the boardwalk. I look at her and laugh, some bystanders giving her a questioning glance. She vanishes into the throngs of people, heading back to our apartment.

"Let's get some ice cream," Jesse says, leading me to the counter.

We order two of the biggest brownie sundaes they have and fight through the crowd to sit on a bench facing the ocean.

"Missed you today," Jesse says. I'd texted him in the early afternoon to tell him I was going out with Jodie. I hadn't told him why, of course.

"Missed you, too."

"Sounds like you two had fun, though. Jodie's such a trip."

"She is."

I don't know if the tension between us is in my imagination or if he can feel it, too. I know it's stemming from me, from the day, and from my questioning of whether or not to be open with Jesse.

"Are you okay?" he asks. Tension is clearly palpable from his stance, too.

I take a bite of my sundae, chewing slowly, savoring every bite. "I am now. But I wasn't."

"What's wrong?"

I take a breath. "Today. It's my wedding date." I look up at the green eyes I've come to trust. I see empathy.

"I'm sorry," he says.

"There's nothing to be sorry about. It is what it is."

"Can't be easy though."

"No. And I hate that it isn't. Because I'm so damn happy. Why is today getting to me so much?"

Tears start to well. A few hours on the boardwalk may have made me feel better, but the hurt is still there, resting out of sight.

Jesse puts his sundae down and takes mine from me. He puts it down as well, taking both my hands in his. His thumb rubs the back of my hand, and I feel the tension slip away.

"Hey, don't be so hard on yourself. Of course today isn't going to be easy. You were married to the man for years. You loved him. I can't imagine what you've been through.

So don't hold back. Feel what you need to feel."

"I don't want you thinking I'm not happy with you."

"I wouldn't think that. Look, neither of us have clean slates when it comes to love. We've both been scarred by the past in one way or another. Those scars are going to ache from time to time. That doesn't take away from what we have, or lessen it. I think it makes it stronger. Because despite those burns we have, we've managed to find this out of the ashes. We've both been hurt, but what we have is strong enough to make us want to push past the hurt and try again. That doesn't mean the past is erased. That doesn't mean our love can make all that pain go away. It means, though, that we can be there for each other and help each other through it. Avery, I love you. Scars and all. Sadness and all. Let me be here for you."

Tears are now flowing, but not from regret or sadness about what I've lost. Tears are falling because of the beauty of the man before me, because of the beauty of a relationship I swore I wouldn't be in.

I don't know if forever is possible. Chris engulfed that view with the flames of his passion for another. Still, staring at Jesse, I think that if forever is possible, it would be most possible with him.

"I love you, too," I whisper into the beachy wind. I rest my head on his shoulder, abandoning our sundaes as we rest in the knowledge of who we are together and a common need to let go of the past.

We sit for a long time, taking in the scene, our beating hearts the only connection between us. We don't have to talk.

We can just be.

That's what I love most about us. There's no pressure or superficiality. Together, we are. That's all there is to it.

When we finally make it back to Jesse's apartment, our kisses aren't filled with the fiery passion they usually are. Instead, they're slow and delicate, as if we're dancing a carefully orchestrated ballet. He carefully peels off my tank top, and I pull his T-shirt over his head. We make love as if we're in no hurry, because really, we're not.

Drifting off to sleep in Jesse's arms, I smile to myself. Life has changed so much in just a year, and it isn't how I imagined it.

With his tattooed arms around me, though, I feel like maybe sometimes life takes us places we could've never dreamed for ourselves because we weren't yet privy to the truth our soul needed.

***

The next morning, Jesse walks me to my apartment before his first appointment. I don't have work until later in the afternoon, but I figure I should go home and spend some time with Jodie. On our walk, I happen to look at my phone for the first time since Dairy Queen.

I have six missed calls from Jodie. My heart leaps in my chest. I hope something isn't wrong.

"Shit, something must be wrong. Jodie called six times last night."

We're rounding the bend toward the apartment.

"We're almost to your apartment. You may as well

see what she needs in person," Jesse says, panic clearly registering in his voice.

As we hurriedly approach our apartment, I fumble with my bag to find my keys. We get to the door, and Jesse follows me in.

"Jodie? Is everything okay? I just got all your ca—" I stop midword because the sight before me is truly horrifying, perhaps worse than I could have imagined.

I now understand why Jodie was so frantic to get hold of me. If only I had picked up the phone.

Chapter Twenty-One

"Avery. Are you just getting in? And who's this? And wow, you've changed your hair. It's… well, it's certainly different."

My mom rises from the sofa as I stand at the door, Jesse at my side. I peer from my mom to my dad, who is still seated on the recliner, to Jodie, who is getting coffee in the kitchen with a look of sheer regret on her face. She mouths, "I tried to warn you."

So this is what was so urgent.

"Mom, when did you guys get in? I didn't know you were coming." My heart flutters as I ignore her questions, trying to get my bearings. I see my dad eyeing Jesse suspiciously, his glance obviously landing on Jesse's visible tattoos.

This is not how I imagined Jesse meeting my parents. This is not how I imagined my parents meeting Jesse—their daughter flying into her apartment at seven in the morning on the day after her wedding anniversary date. Hopefully Mom is so caught up on my new hairstyle that she doesn't take time to realize it's definitely sex hair.

"Last night. We wanted to surprise you. We thought it would be a rough day for you. Obviously, it wasn't too rough." Mom smells of the expensive perfume from the department store. She's wearing a dress that probably cost more than our monthly rent. She looks at me with the disapproving eye I've seen so many times before.

"Sorry I wasn't here. We were out."

Jesse steps forward, extending a hand to my mother. "Hi, Mrs. Johannas. I'm Jesse Pearce. Nice to meet you."

Mom shakes his hand silently, her condescending look certainly not just in my imagination. Dad finally gets to his feet and also shakes Jesse's hand.

"So, are you staying close by?" I ask, trying to figure out how to best handle the situation. I certainly hope they didn't stay here last night. Poor Jodie. I owe her fifteen rounds of drinks.

"Yes. After your dear friend informed us of where you were and we realized you weren't coming home last night, we checked into our hotel down the street. We came back this morning hoping you'd be home."

I feel my face blush. I'm an adult. I shouldn't have to defend myself to my parents. It's still just a little awkward, and not what I had in mind for their first trip down here.

"How about we go get some breakfast?" Jodie joyfully suggests, probably sensing the tension. "We can all get to know each other."

"I *am* hungry," Dad says.

"Midsummer Nights sound good? I'm sure Lysander will

let us in early, and Georgina would be glad to make some breakfast. Then your parents can see where you work."

"Sounds great," I say, although it doesn't sound great at all. I can hardly wait to hear what my parents have to say about it.

"I'll call Lysander and tell him to get us a table ready."

"Thank you, darling," Mom says, and I'm reminded of how much I hate it when she uses that word.

"So, how long are you staying?" I nonchalantly ask, hoping she'll say a day.

"Oh, I don't know. A few days at least," she answers, and I feel the happiness from last night wane.

"Great. We'll get to know each other," Jesse says, trying to stay positive and probably trying to impress my parents.

I purposely haven't talked a whole lot about them, but I can't shield Jesse from them any longer. He's about to find out just how aggravating they can be.

Don't get me wrong. I love them. But loving them and agreeing with their… attitudes… are two different things.

And loving them and knowing they're going to rip Jesse apart—that's a completely different story altogether.

***

Jesse calls Brett to get him to cover his appointment for him. I insist he doesn't have to do that, but he won't hear otherwise. I know it shouldn't matter that my parents are here. It's not like I'm a teenager asking for my dad's approval. I can't help but be a little stressed though. I feel a bit like Jesse's on trial, and that I have to prove to my parents I didn't rush into a mistake.

I feel like no matter how great Jesse is, he'll never win them over. They've been against my move here from the beginning. Adding a new man to the picture is only going to solidify their hatred of this new life I've owned.

We walk to Midsummer Nights, Mom chattering on about her latest trip to the spa and about how stressed Dad's been. We listen to her fill the walk with discussions of the weather and traffic. She talks about how her flip-flops are hurting her feet, about the new stray cat in the neighborhood, and everything else that pops in her head. No one gets a word in, which is fine with me. I revel in not talking, in just walking beside Jesse, holding hands.

When we get to Midsummer Nights, Jesse holds the door for all of us.

"Oh, wow. This is such a cute place," Mom says. I can't read her expression to tell if there's a hint of sarcasm underneath it.

"Yeah, it's pretty great. We love working here, right, Avery?" Jodie asks.

"We do. Lysander is amazing. And they have great food," I respond, meaning it. I'm glad my parents are going to see where I work and the friends I've made. Maybe now they'll realize this isn't just a stage I'm going through or a whim. It's my life, and I'm happy.

"Wow, coming to work early," Lysander jokes when we walk through the door.

"You wish," Jodie says, flopping into the huge, round booth in the corner reserved for large parties. Today, we qualify.

We all scooch into the enormous booth, but still sit a little closer than I'd like to be in this situation. Jesse ends up between me and my mom, and Jodie is to my left. We hand my parents menus, none of us needing them.

"So, Jesse, tell me about your work. What do you do?" Mom asks as she peruses the menu.

"I'm a tattoo artist," he says.

"Oh, I see," my dad responds.

"He owns a tattoo parlor. Not just any parlor, though. He's one of the best in town," I say, hating that I sound like I'm defending Jesse's job. I hate that my parents make me feel like I have to.

"Yeah, that's actually how they met," Jodie pipes in.

"Oh, wow." Mom eyes me, before turning to my dad. "So, I think I'm going to get pancakes."

In my mother's world, this is her way of saying she doesn't approve and that she thinks I'm an idiot. I've spent enough time with her to know this is her way of giving Jesse the cold shoulder.

I try not to let it get to me. Of course Mom isn't going to like him, because if she admits he's good for me, she's basically condoning me staying here. She's not ready to admit I've made a good decision. She's not ready to let me go. More than that, I don't think she's ready to let go of the perfect image she had for my life—and the fact this doesn't fit the bill.

We continue small talk about the weather forecast and the hash browns. Eventually, Lysander himself takes our order.

"Mr. and Mrs. Johannas, I just want to say it's been a pleasure having your daughter here. She's a stand-up girl."

"Yes, I agree. Although I wouldn't get used to her. I'm sure this is just a temporary job for her, with her having a degree and all."

"Mom, really?" I say, giving her dagger eyes. I look to Lysander, shaking my head. He just smiles at me and gives me a look that says he understands. I sigh, frustrated already with this whole scenario. Still, we put in our orders, and Lysander heads to the kitchen.

Jodie and Jesse are both pretty quiet. I'm guessing they can sense the tension. Great. I finally find happiness with Jesse, and now my parents are going to send him running for the hills.

As if he can read my mind, he squeezes my hand under the table. I turn and smile at him. He gets it. He's not going anywhere. We just need to make it through today.

"So how was yesterday for you? Was it tough, sweetie?" Mom asks as Dad sips his coffee, probably trying to avoid this awkward conversation. He's never been one to talk about emotions.

"A little. But I'm okay."

"I don't think you could possibly be okay. He was such a huge part of our life. It's just a shame it ended the way it did."

I'm silent. There's nothing I can say to this.

"So did Avery tell you about her amazing painting?" Jodie says, probably trying to help out by changing the subject.

"You're painting?" Dad asks, seemingly thankful for the subject change.

"Just on the side."

"Are you kidding? You get like five calls a week," Jodie pipes in.

"You're amazing," Jesse says, his green eyes peering into mine. He turns to my mom. "She is seriously good. You should swing by the tattoo parlor and see her work."

Mom's face is unmoved. "Maybe at some point I could. It's good to have a hobby, I suppose," she says.

I feel the cut of her words. I try to remind myself this is who she is. She's always been this way. I can't change her. Being away from her these past few months, fleeing from so much of the family drama, has made me realize that moving here has been freeing in more ways than one.

Mom does cool down over breakfast, though. She actually laughs at a few of Jesse's jokes, asks Jodie about her writing, and even appears moved when Jesse tells the story about why he opened a tattoo shop. I calm down, thinking I'm just being hard on Mom. This is a big change for her. I get that.

As frustrating as she can be, as overbearing as she can be, I love her. She's my mom, and she's always been there for me. Her intentions are in the right place.

So when breakfast is finished and Jesse says his goodbyes to head to work, I'm shocked by the shift in tone. Once Jodie's headed back to the kitchen to talk to Lysander, and Jesse's out of sight, the true words surface.

"You aren't getting serious with him, are you? Tell me

you're not," Mom barks as soon as the door closes behind him.

"Mom, what if I am?"

"He's not good for you. He's a tattoo artist, for God's sake. You need something bigger in your life. You're a go-getter. Don't settle. Don't rebound."

My blood boils now. "Are you kidding me? Is anyone good enough for you? Oh, I'm sorry, hotshot Chris was good enough for you. And look how that turned out. Mom, I've started a new life for myself, and I love it."

"You're a waitress, Avery. Really? After all that schooling, this is what you choose?" She motions toward the Shakespeare poster near us.

"Yes. I'm happy here. I thought you'd be happy that I'm happy, but I guess not." I toss down my napkin and scooch toward my dad, who graciously lets me out of the booth. I storm out of Midsummer Nights, tears forming.

I feel like I'm seventeen again. I know I shouldn't let this get to me.

But it does. I wanted her to like him. I wanted her to be happy that I've found a new sense of happiness. Maybe if I'm being honest, I wanted some sort of validation that I've done well for myself. I know it's stupid. I know I should be making my own decisions and owning them. I guess after spending my whole life seeking her approval, things haven't changed as much as I would like. I still haven't let go of the need to make her proud of me—which is a difficult battle.

I wanted Mom to see I've done a good thing here and that I've found something special. I guess I should've known better.

Because just like Chris, my mom only sees me one way. She sees the Avery she wants to see, and this version of me doesn't fit with her view.

I storm out onto the boardwalk, kick off my shoes, and head down to the beach. There are already some tanners and some volleyball players claiming their pieces of beach. I head down to the water, my sanctuary. I remind myself to breathe.

I stand for a while gawking at the water, wondering how things got so complicated. Last night was the best night of my life. Why do I let this taint my mood? Why am I letting my mom's opinions get to me?

"I truly think she means well, although she has a funny way of showing it," a deep voice says. I turn to see my dad, also barefoot, standing beside me. "It's beautiful here. Great view."

I smile. "It's just frustrating. She can be so difficult sometimes."

"You're telling me." Dad chuckles. "I know she's overbearing. I honestly think she just misses you. She has a crappy way of showing it, I know. I think she's worried you're rushing into a life here, that you're settling into something as a rebound."

I sigh. "But I'm not."

We stand for a while, admiring the waves crashing into each other. A few kids shriek and run, one chasing the other with a sand crab. I laugh, and so does my dad.

"Listen, Avery, I want to talk to you about something.

Please just hear me out, okay?"

I nod. My dad's always been more rational, more levelheaded. I heed his words more than my mom's.

"The truth is, we didn't just come here to check on you. I wanted to talk to you about something."

I feel like this is going to be a pivotal moment, a pivotal question. My dad's voice seems to waver with uncertainty.

"Okay," I respond, waiting for him to drop a bombshell.

"I'm retiring. It's time for me to move on to the next phase of life, to relax a little."

"Wow. How soon?"

"A few months. I need to get some things in order."

"Okay." I kind of know where this might be going, but I don't want to jump to conclusions.

"I want you to take over the firm, Avery."

"Dad, I—"

"Just listen. You know the business. You're family. You should be in charge. I know you need some more experience, but I can help you. I can get you ready to take over."

I look at the waves again, soaking in my dad's words. Not long ago, this would have been news I would have been eager to hear. This would've been the opportunity of a lifetime. This would have prompted a champagne celebration with Chris and animated talk about the future. This would have been what I was searching for.

Now the words are just confusing. They make me feel trapped between the life I'm supposed to live and the life I want to live. Suddenly, I feel enmeshed in the life I had and the life I have. How can I reconcile the two?

I'm happy here. I'm building a life. Sure, it's simple and nothing like my old life. But that's sort of the point. It's easy and relaxed. It's walks on the beach with Henry and Jake, and nights at the carnival with Jodie. It's ice-cream dates with Jesse, and parasailing adventures. It's everything that stuffy firm didn't give me. It's everything Chris, Pittsburgh, and my old life couldn't be.

But what my dad is offering isn't something to toss into the wind, either. His offer is an offer of financial security. It's the chance to be someone important, to be successful in a very physical sense of the word. It's the chance to lead and to be powerful. It's the chance to rise to my potential. It's the chance to be loyal to my family and carry on my dad's legacy. It's an opportunity to be a good daughter and to help out those I love. It's something that at one point I thought I wanted. It's something I think I really did want at one point—but what about now?

"Dad, I don't know. I'm happy here."

"But you were happy at home once, too. I know this whole Chris thing threw you off course. Please, Avery, don't let his mistakes change the trajectory of your entire life. Don't lower your goals because of him. I know this life is making you happy right now, and I understand its appeal. But tell me, Avery, is this enough? You're a go-getter. You've always wanted to climb the ladder. Will you regret it if you say no to this?"

"I don't know," I mutter before I can censor my words. Because it's the truth, if I'm being honest. I don't know what I'm going to feel down the road. Either way, I'm going to leave something behind.

"Just think about it, okay? I don't need an answer today or even tomorrow. But I want you to decide for yourself. I want you to make the decision that's right for you. Forget about Chris. Forget about what Jesse wants. Forget about trying to live a different life, and live a life you actually want. Live a life that isn't going to leave you with regrets. I think if you're really honest, that life could be running the firm. Selfishly, I want it to be that choice. So does your mom. But Avery, I want you to make the decision that's right for you."

I feel tears trickling because of the momentousness of his words, but also because of the confusion they've brought.

Last night, I finally had a breakthrough. I finally felt without a doubt that I'm right where I belong. But what if Dad's right? What if this isn't the life that will make me happy in the long run? What if having this freedom, this life, means giving up on a dream I used to have? A dream I might even still have, at least to some extent?

And so, yet again I feel tossed out to sea, two life rafts floating toward me.

And for the first time since coming here, I absolutely don't know which one is the one I should reach for.

Chapter Twenty-Two

My parents stay for two more days. We all go to dinner the next night, and things smooth out with Jesse. I feel like he wins them over, even making my mom laugh over his joke about the president. Things are on the up. Of course, maybe it's just because Dad told Mom he thinks he got through to me.

For a few days, I let it go, trying not to think about the decision I have to make. I want to go back to being the Avery in Jesse's bed, thinking about the possibilities here, not having to think about giving up an entire business and financial future.

The Wednesday after my parents leave, Jesse texts me after my shift at work.

Jesse: Coming to get you. Get ready for some action.

I giggle at his text, which is the worst pickup line or innuendo I've ever heard. Still, I toss on my favorite jeans and a cozy flannel, the chilly air necessitating warmer clothes. Who knows what he has in mind, but it's best to be prepared for some time outside.

When he picks me up a few hours later, he's also wearing jeans and a flannel.

"Wow. Twins?" I laugh, gesturing toward our red flannels.

"You two are just adorable," Jodie says, coming into the living room from her nap in her room. She's holding Sebastian, who is purring so loudly I can hear him across the room.

"Should I change?" I ask, not really sure what the protocol is when you match your boyfriend.

"I'm insulted. You don't want to match me? I'm the king of style."

I snicker, shrug, and then wave goodbye to Jodie as I follow him out the door. He grabs my hand, and despite the chill in the air, despite the scent of fall creeping into me, I warm.

"So where to?" I ask, curious.

"Somewhere with lots of action. I told you."

"I have no idea what that means."

"You're about to find out."

I smile, shaking my head. With Jesse, you never know where you're headed.

I love that about him.

A few minutes later and after some discussion about the latest tattoo drama, we arrive at our destination.

Funland.

"Really?" I grin. Inside, I'm jumping up and down a little. I haven't been to an arcade since I was young.

There's just something about those neon lights, those beeping games, and the music that takes me back. Nostalgia courses through my veins as we walk under the lit-up sign.

With the summer sun fading into fall and the tourists mostly dispersed, it's desolate on the boardwalk. We've got the place to ourselves, other than a guy named Steve working the prize counter.

"Are you ready to get your butt kicked in every game in the arcade?" Jesse asks.

I scoff at him. "Are you kidding? I was the arcade champ in my day. I even earned enough tickets to get the sno-cone machine in sixth grade."

"We'll see about that. I'm a pro at Skee Ball."

"I bet I'll get more tickets than you."

"You're on. What's the bet?"

I grin, pretending to rub my chin. "Oh, I'm sure we can think of something to play for." I give him a purposely creepy wink.

"Not getting what you're saying," he says teasingly.

I lean in and whisper in his ear. Steve is eyeing us from the counter. I blush a little just thinking about Steve overhearing what I'm saying.

I'm not one to talk dirty. But I guess I'll blame it on the neon lights and the crazy music coming from the DDR machine.

Jesse turns a bit red as well. "You're on."

"Game on," I reply.

He shakes his head.

"What?"

"It's just, don't get me wrong, I like your bet. But we are in a kids' arcade. Jesus, woman. I didn't think you were so…."

"Frisky? Racy?"

"Bold. Let's go with bold," he says, winking.

Inspired by his word choice, I grab his hand and yank him toward the Skee Ball game after we claim some tokens.

We spend the afternoon laughing like two children, racing around the arcade as Steve keeps an awkward eye on us. Inspired by the atmosphere, I forget about all the adult decisions I have to make, my life's path, and the choice set before me. Instead, I focus on the moment presented by the cheesy arcade games and gorgeous guy to play them with.

By the end of the evening, we are both battling over ticket counts, claiming our prizes—a gorgeous "gemstone" necklace for me, and a cooler for Jesse.

It's not until we get back to his place, though, that we can settle the real bet.

I claim my prize, going with my new motto of bold, grinning ear to ear as Jesse pays up. *I'm right where I belong*. This is happiness in its sheerest form.

We drift off to sleep in each other's arms, and I feel like I'm home.

But in the middle of the night, I wake up. Jesse is sleeping on his side of the bed, me on my back. I stare at the hairline crack in Jesse's ceiling, thinking about our wonderful night together and wondering if it could really last forever. I love him. I do. I love how he inspires me to have fun, to be in the moment, and to go to an arcade on a random Wednesday to battle over tickets. I love that he makes me want to be adventurous, to be like the ocean breeze and follow every whim. I love the feel of his hands on my body and the knowledge that he's right beside me, an arm's length away.

I love everything about Jesse Pearce.

Still, lying here with the alarm clock telling me it's almost 3:00 a.m., my mind starts to drift away from the warmth of the bed and the feel of his body beside me. I start to think about the future and the past. I think about how not long ago, another man was beside me in a very different bed. I think about how I was certain it would last forever.

I was certain he was sheer happiness once.

That happiness faded. What if this fades, too? What if our relationship, like the summer sun, fades into a colder, more bitter season? What if the love and energy we feel now settles into something less exciting? What if the distance between us in this bed keeps getting vaster?

More than that, I start to think about me and who I am. I think about the woman I was when I came here, and the promises I made. What would the old Avery say about this? What would the Avery from a few months ago say about this? I've broken my vow, and for what? Love doesn't work out. I love him. I trust him. But I've been there before. Am I being a fool? Can I really give up the career opportunity of a lifetime for my heart's desire? Can I basically abandon my family and their legacy to stay here? Then again, can I leave behind the new legacy for myself I'm building to return home to a life I so desperately wanted to get away from? Am I ready to abandon the new, free Avery I've uncovered, who paints and has a great group of friends? I don't know if I can just leave this creative, openhearted Avery here in the sands of Ocean City and go back home, pretending I never lived this life. Then again, I don't know if I can forever abandon the Avery I used to be and the family that, despite their overbearing tendencies, I love.

What's the right answer? How do I choose between my family by blood and the family I've found here? How do I choose indefinitely between the Avery of the past and the unknown Avery I could be in the future?

The more I stare at the hairline crack, the more I feel like the bliss of a few hours ago is dissipating into the chilly night air. I can't help but feel like the crack is growing and the doubt is falling right through the ceiling. Things that were clear a few hours ago are murky again.

Most of all, I feel like the man beside me might be slipping away, even if he doesn't know it yet.

Chapter Twenty-Three

I know I should tell Jesse what's going on. I should let him in on my parents' offer, if nothing else, than to just be honest.

But I'm afraid. I'm afraid he'll see right through my "I'm sure I'm not taking the offer" words. I'm afraid he'll see my hesitation and go running away. I'm afraid he'll give up on us before I've even left.

I know I can't keep such a momentous thing to myself. Instead of telling Jesse in the morning, though, I kiss him goodbye at my door, head inside, and decide to do the next best thing.

I tell my group of friends who are really more like family. Luckily, the opportunity presents itself immediately, since Lysander and Reed are having lunch with Jodie when I get back to the apartment.

"Hey, stranger. Want some tomato soup and grilled cheese?" Reed asks from the stove.

I smile. "No thanks."

"Don't give us that look. You know you love grilled

cheese and tomato soup. Don't act like you're too old," Jodie says, a huge piece of sandwich in her mouth.

"It is sort of the meal of five-year-olds, but I'm not judging," I say, tossing my hands in the air.

I plop onto a stool at the island beside Lysander, who is also eating.

"So what's new?" Lysander asks.

I sigh, resting my head in my hands, not sure how much to divulge.

"Oh no. Don't tell me there's trouble in paradise with the tattooed hunk," Reed asks, also taking a seat. Sebastian is meowing at his feet as Henry puts his drooly face in my lap.

"Not exactly."

"Spill. Come on. We need details," Reed encourages.

So I lay it all out there. The offer from my parents. The financial aspects of it. My love for Jesse. The sense of freedom I've found here. My sense of family loyalty. How much I hate myself for even considering the offer. How guilty I feel for letting my dad down.

How completely and utterly confused I truly am.

"Wow. That's intense," Jodie says, shaking her head once I'm finished.

"So what are you leaning toward?" Reed asks.

Emotionally exhausted from telling the tale, I shrug. "I love him. I really do. And I love the life I've found here with all of you and with my painting. I'm so happy. But I'm afraid I'll regret giving this up. I feel like I can't just let my family legacy die. I trained for this. My dad's counting on me."

"But honey, didn't you give it all up for a reason? Didn't you come here because you weren't happy?" Reed says pragmatically.

And he's right. It makes sense. "Yes. And that's why I don't understand why this is so hard for me. I wish I wasn't thinking about wanting to take up the offer. But I guess it's just that I worked for this for so long. Not long ago, this would have been exactly what I wanted."

"But you're a different person now, in a good way," Lysander says. "You've changed."

"Yes, but I don't think that makes it easy to just sever ties with who you were before," Reed observes. "I've been there. I get it. Sometimes, I wonder what could have happened if I had stayed in my career. I've thought about how my degree, my experience is sitting there."

"So you regret coming here?" I ask, a little surprised by his words.

He looks over to Lysander with a grin. "Never. Because even though I did give up some of my old dreams to come here, I also found new ones, ones that have made me happier than I could've ever imagined. Life is always about sacrifice, Avery. It's always a give and take. You just have to be able to be honest about what you're willing to give up."

"Yeah, and besides, Jesse is freaking hot. Why isn't anyone talking about that? Guys like him aren't just ripe for the picking, trust me," Jodie adds in typical Jodie fashion.

I grin. "It's not all about looks, you know."

She rolls her eyes. "Oh, please. Why don't you just take Jesse with you? Then you can have money and the hottie."

"Well, there's a thought," Lysander says. "Although we can't give you up." He reaches to touch my hand across the island.

"Yeah, we would have to go back to knitting without our pet project to work on," Reed says, and I laugh.

"We're not kidding," Jodie says. "Plus, I'd be poor and have to find a rich man to help pay the rent."

"Gold digger," Reed says pointedly, and I laugh again.

"I don't think I could ask Jesse to give up his tattoo parlor. That wouldn't be fair."

"Please. The man is crazy about you. He'd move his tattoo parlor to Antarctica for you."

"I wouldn't ask him to do that. He couldn't do that."

"Wait, you have told him about this, right?" Jodie asks. "You've talked to him about your dad's offer?"

I avert my eyes.

"Are you serious? What the hell is wrong with you?" she says. "You need to tell him. Either way, you should talk to him about it."

"She's right," Lysander says. "Besides, maybe he can help you."

I know they're correct. I know I need to stop putting it off.

"I guess I'm just scared it will ruin things."

Reed walks over to me, putting an arm around my shoulders. "Then maybe you have your answer after all. Maybe it's not so hard," he practically whispers, and a rogue tear slides down my face.

"Love you guys," I say, meaning it. I came here not

knowing if I'd even find a single friend in this place. Instead, I found three friends who are becoming more and more like family.

Leaving here wouldn't just be leaving Jesse. It would be leaving all of this behind, everything good I've made for myself.

"Okay, this is turning into a sappy television drama. I can't take it. Can we please do something fun? Some of us don't even have a hottie to think about walking away from," Jodie interrupts.

"Let's go find Jodie a hottie. What do you say, Avery?"

I wipe the tear away and brush the momentousness of the moment aside, nodding in agreement as I get up to go slip into one of my "going out" shirts.

***

After a wild night where we do, in fact, find Jodie a hottie—who turns out to be gay—I tuck myself into bed, ready to let go of the alcohol haze and the decisions swirling in my head. Before I can even blink, the sun is shining through the window and my phone is buzzing with an incoming call.

"Hello?" my crackling voice says.

"Avery? You sound rough. Are you getting sick?"

I wipe the sleep from my eyes, rolling over to pet Henry as I face a conversation with my mother.

"No, Mom. I'm just tired."

"It's eleven in the morning. I'll tell you, your schedule these days is something."

I roll my eyes like the insolent teenager I once was,

flopping onto my back now to stare at the ceiling. I breathe into the phone, hoping my silence sends the message that I'm not amused by her comments.

"So, I'm just calling to see when you're coming back."

"Mom, I don't know if I am."

"Really, Avery? You're not sure yet? What is there to think about?"

"It's complicated. I'm happy here."

There's a pause. I wait patiently for the derision that is sure to fly out of her mouth. I wait for her to chide me about being responsible and making good decisions. I wait to hear her talk to me like the angry teenager she sometimes thinks I still am.

She doesn't, though. In fact, I'm almost taken aback when her voice is soft and restrained.

"Avery, I love you. And I know sometimes I'm tough on you. This past year has been challenging. You've gone through a lot, and I'm sorry for that. I just don't want to see you pass up this opportunity because you're scared to come back. I don't want to see you throw away such a huge career move for something that's making you happy right now. I know you're creating a life down there. I see that now. But is it a life that will sustain you forever? Is it something to build a foundation for the future on? Or is it just that it's different, and after what Chris did to you, you want to claim anything that you can say is your own?"

I bite my cracking, chapped lips, pondering her words, my stomach wrenching either from last night's booze or the haunting truth resonating in her words.

"I don't know, Mom."

"Honey, please just don't do what you did before. Don't make this about a man. Make this about you. We miss you. Your family is here, Avery. We're here for you. Come back where you belong."

We talk for a few more minutes about trivial things, but the whole time, I'm thinking about Mom's words.

I think about how not long ago, her words were exactly what I'd promised myself. I think about how those green eyes swept me up and made me turn my back on my promise.

Most of all, I consider that maybe my mom, who drives me batshit crazy at times, may be undoubtedly right about everything.

Chapter Twenty-Four

"You're quiet," Jesse says as we stroll along the beach, Henry and Jake in tow, a few days later. The wind is stronger than usual, and the boardwalk is all but empty, only a few haunts favorited by the locals remaining open. Pretty soon, even Midsummer will face the fall and winter lull.

Wrapping my hoodie around me tighter, I shrug. In truth, I *have* been quiet, mostly because my dad's offer keeps twirling in my head. At first, I felt like it was obviously a "no." I was happy. I left Pennsylvania to find something new for myself. I've found it. Why the hell would I give it up?

But then I think about all I've worked for. I think about the degree sitting in a desk drawer, and about a future of waiting tables and painting. I think about letting Dad down, about letting our family down. Is that what I truly want? Am I going to look back someday and regret this decision?

It's a momentous decision. Either way I sacrifice. The question is—what do I choose?

The biggest pull for me to stay, for me to give up the family business, is the man walking hand in hand with me now. He won my heart back. He's made me believe I can love again, even if I'm scared. I don't know exactly where this thing with him will go, but I'm not ready to let it go.

A part of me thinks moving back to Pittsburgh doesn't have to mean the end of us. Long-distance relationships are possible, right? The movies make them look possible. Rationally, I tell myself I can have it all. Emotionally, I know it won't be the same. To go back to Pittsburgh is to say goodbye to Jesse.

When I came here, I told myself I wouldn't live for a man. I wouldn't let my feelings for another dictate my choices. Still, it isn't that cut-and-dried. It isn't that easy, even if I want it to be. If I were sticking to my promise, I'd say goodbye to whatever this is with Jesse and pursue what would make me the best version of myself.

Then again, is going back to Pittsburgh what would make me the best version? Is being financially stable and successful in the career related to my degree what I actually want? Even if Jesse weren't in the picture, would this be the answer?

The thing is, Jesse is in the picture. I can't remove him from the situation, and I don't want to. Although I came here to find freedom, he's undoubtedly laid claim to my heart with his eyes, with his lips, with his unwavering support of the new Avery. I love him.

So I say it. "I love you." It's a beachside confession, mostly for myself. I need to hear the words aloud, to remember where I'm at in my life, to remember how true they are, no matter how hard I tried to fight it.

"I love you too," he says, wrapping me into his arms. "Do you think your parents like me?"

It's a double-edged question, one I'm not sure how to answer. "I think so. But honestly, I'm not sure if they like themselves sometimes. They're difficult."

"Yeah, your mom's definitely not one to hide her feelings."

"That's for sure. Or her agenda."

"What do you mean?" He pulls back, looking at me. Henry is barking at Jake a little ways down the beach. The two will roughhouse for a few moments and then simultaneously plop over in the sand. We've done this walk enough to know their habits and to know we don't have to worry about them running away.

"Nothing. It's nothing," I say, trying to brush it off and avoid the conversation. I don't want Jesse worrying I'm considering the offer.

Am I considering it? I don't even know. I exhale.

"Doesn't seem like nothing. Just tell me."

I eye him, wondering if I should give in. I decide, though, there's no use hiding it. "My dad is retiring. He offered to hand the firm over to me."

"Wow," Jesse says, running a hand through his hair, shock on his face. "That's huge."

"Yeah. At one point, I would have been ecstatic."

Jesse hesitates before asking, "And now?"

It's my turn to pause. I look into his eyes, pleading with

me for the truth. "I don't know. It's a big deal. It's our family business."

"But if you took it, you'd have to move?"

"Yeah. It's too much to handle from here."

Jesse exhales softly, still staring at me. "You should take it."

"What? No. Of course not. I'm happy here."

"I know. But it's your family business. How can you give that up? It's a big thing."

"I don't want to leave. I love it here, love everything about being here. I've created this new life for myself, a life I love. I've found people I love. How can I just leave it all?"

Jesse slumps down to the sand, taking a seat. Jake and Henry, as predicted, are worn out, sleeping on their sides, panting. I slink down beside Jesse, staring at the horizon.

We sit in silence for a while, both mulling over the news and what it means. I think about how much I like the feel of him beside me, of seeing the same view he's seeing. I think about how I'd give up anything to be with him. I think about how we shouldn't even be talking about this.

"Jesse, I'm not taking it. I'm staying. I can't just leave everything behind. I can't leave you, what we have, behind."

Jesse is still quiet, still staring. I almost think he's gone somewhere else mentally, like he's ignoring me. Finally, he speaks.

"I was four the first time I realized my mom was gone. I mean, of course I knew it before then. But when I was four, it really hit me what it meant."

I stare at him, not sure what this has to do with anything.

Still, the serious look on his face tells me this is something he needs to say, so I listen.

"It was my birthday party. Dad didn't have a lot of money, of course, but he'd scraped together enough to have a cake and ice cream for a few of my preschool friends. I remember sitting there, staring at my cake, not wanting to eat it. I thought that if I didn't take a bite of that cake, she'd come. I thought if I could just wait a few more minutes, if I could just not take a bite of that cake, Mom would come back. It was my *birthday*. Surely she'd show. I felt like if I took a bite of the cake, though, it was over. She wasn't going to come. I know now it was irrational and made no sense. But at the time, it was real to me."

"I'm sorry."

He goes on, ignoring me, needing to finish telling the story. "She never showed, and I never took a bite of that cake. I couldn't. Dad tried to console me, to tell me I had plenty of people who loved me, and that Mom didn't want to leave. I didn't understand. And when I did understand years later, the sadness turned to something else. It turned to hate. I hated her. I hated her for leaving us. I hated her for not showing up. I hated her for walking out."

I turn now to rub his arm, to squeeze his hand. I can see, even now, the pain on his face. I can see the sense of loss.

"I still hate what she did to us, especially to my dad. I hate that I spent so many years wishing on a fake star that she'd come home. I *hate* that. But over the years, I've come to realize something. We just weren't what she had in mind for her life. We weren't the dream she had. I hate that we weren't. I hate that we weren't enough for her. But then, I also can't blame her for pursuing her dreams, even if they were selfish. She just wanted to live a different life. I don't understand it. I don't like it. But I can't hold it against her, because I don't know what it's like to be trapped in a life you don't want."

"You should have been her dream."

"Yes. But sometimes people need more than what we think they should want. They need something else. It isn't always about love or about being with someone. Sometimes it's about needing something else, somewhere else, deep in your core."

His words shake me. I'm afraid of where this is going.

"Avery, I love you with every fiber of my being. I didn't want to love you. I didn't want to lose my heart to you, because I was terrified it would get broken. I was terrified that like so many other women in my life, you'd leave."

"I won't. I'm not."

"Listen, please," he says, kissing my cheek. "I was so afraid of losing you that I didn't want to love you. But I did anyway. I fell in love with you. I want nothing more than to spend my days here, right here, you by my side, staring at the horizon. But that's not fair. It's not fair that because I'm afraid to lose you, you should stay here. It's not fair that I should make you stare at the horizon when beyond it, there's so much more for you."

"Jesse, I don't want what's beyond it. I want what's right here, what I've found."

"But I think you do want what's beyond. It was your dream.

And yes, you've found a new version of you, of your life, that you can appreciate these past few months. You've found a love between us that you can trust in. Deep down, I think a piece of you knows that what you have in Pittsburgh, what you could have, is so much more. It's what you worked so hard for. I can't let our love hold you back. You need to go."

"I don't want to leave you."

"And I don't want to hold you here. I don't want you deciding your future based on us. I don't want you to feel like my mom did—trapped. I want you to be free to explore your wildest dreams, even if that means I have to let you go."

Tears are coming to my eyes. I stare at those green eyes, the ones that opened up the entire world for me over the course of a few months. In them, I now see something else.

Loss.

I'm losing him, whether I go or not.

"Jesse, I love you."

"I love you, too. And that's why you need to go."

I want to argue and fight. I want to shove him, to tell him he's wrong.

I want to beg him to come with me, but the unspoken words between us tell me this isn't fair. I know what his parlor, what this dream means to him. As much as he can't ask me to give up my dreams, I can't ask him to give up his.

So instead, I accept his kiss, a gentle, hesitant kiss. I feel his lips on mine for what could be the last time.

A part of me wants to get up and pull him back, to make him see how wrong he is. I don't, though. I don't know why.

Maybe it's fear. Maybe it's because I'm hurt that he'd let me go so easily.

Or maybe it's because a piece of me thinks he might just be right.

So when Jesse Pearce gathers Jake, pats Henry goodbye, and dutifully marches through the sand toward his home without me, I turn and look back at the horizon. The sun is fading slowly, and the day is turning into night. My days as the wild and free beach girl feel like they're long gone. The stars are shining with the truth.

I opened my heart back up to Jesse Pearce, but that doesn't mean forever will be ours.

Chapter Twenty-Five

Days pass. Long, agonizing days that shoot me back into a state of remorse and confusion. I miss the hell out of him, and it's only been a few days.

Worst of all, I still don't think going home is what I want, despite what Jesse said. Why does every decision have to be so damn complicated? Why can't this be like a movie where the heroine knows exactly what she should do when every choice comes her way?

Of course, in my flannel pajamas and with a scrunchie in my hair, I'm not quite a heroine. I'm just a mess.

"You know, you could put an end to this misery," Jodie says, plopping on the couch beside me and handing me a cup of coffee. It's late, and we're both done with our shifts at Midsummer. I spent the night trying to paint on a sad excuse for a smile, which Jodie told me looked more like a constipation face. Lysander also noticed because he gave me an extra break complete with a Love-in-Idleness.

"We've talked about this."

"And I've told you you're making a mistake," she says. "You know you don't want to go back home, or you'd be there. You know what you have with Jesse is more than some fling. You know your heart won't let you just leave him. So why don't you tell him?"

I shake my head, staring at the coffee table as I warm my hands on my mug of coffee. "He didn't fight for me. He wants to let me go. He was willing to let me go."

Jodie puts a hand on my knee, shaking me. "He's just scared. He loves you. But he doesn't want to hold you back. Look at his past. He's been there. He's had two women walk out on him because they weren't happy with him. I think he's just afraid if he tells you to stay, you'll regret it and hold it against him. He's afraid you'll walk out eventually."

"But I'm scared, too. I'm scared he'll walk out. I'm terrified to give my heart back to a man who was okay with letting me go. If he was okay with me leaving, maybe it wasn't real in the first place."

"In his warped mind, he probably thought he was doing the right thing. He thought you needed him to let you go. It makes no sense. Neither of you make sense right now. You love each other. Stop being scared. Stop letting fear in the way. Stop pretending this is about deciding whether or not to take your dad's offer. This is about you needing an out. It's about both of you finding an out so you have an excuse not to be completely, one hundred percent in. You're afraid of getting hurt."

"I just love him so much that it scares me."

"Then cling to him. Make it work. Jump in, Avery. Not

halfway. Not in the shallow end. Jump the hell in. No matter what you do in life, you have to make choices. There's always a risk you're going to regret it. But which will you regret more—letting go of the family business, or letting go of Jesse?"

I stare, not answering her, silence doing the talking for me.

It's him. It's always been him. I came to Ocean City swearing I wouldn't fall in love again. Yet, it feels like all along, I was meant to fall for him. I was meant to find him.

I came here to find the new Avery, but it was Jesse who helped me figure out who she was. From our spontaneous trips to the beach to parasailing to the painting business, he helped me figure out who I want to be. He makes me who I want to be. I am only the new Avery with him by my side, *because* he's by my side.

It's not that a man is dictating my life or defining me. It's that this man makes me want to live my life and define myself.

Chapter Twenty-Six

"I don't know what you're doing at work," Lysander says the next night, Tuesday night. "Jodie filled me in that you realize what a fool you're being. Why the hell aren't you having hot make-up sex with Jesse right now?"

"Well hello to you too, boss. Glad I showed up like a responsible adult," I say, teasing.

"No seriously. What are you doing? Get the hell over there," Reed says. He's sitting at the bar, drinking a martini and eating some fried mushrooms.

"I just… I don't know what to do or how to handle this. I don't know if he's going to feel the same way. I'm scared."

"If I hear that word one more time," Jodie teases, snagging a mushroom from Reed's basket. "I told her to run over there last night. I told her to go over this morning. I told her to text him. The woman's impossible."

I sigh, blowing a strand of hair out of my face. She's right. I am impossible. But every time I play in my head what to say, what to do, I freeze. It just felt like Jesse left

Inked Hearts

things so final. Am I prepared to go back and tell him it was a mistake? What if he disagrees? What if the past few days have given him a sense of clarity that doesn't match mine?

"Well, it's Tuesday, lucky for you. So he should be in any moment," Jodie says, winking before heading back to work.

She's right. I knew this was coming. I knew Tuesday was coming.

The rest of the night, I'm an anxious ball of nerves, trying to focus on work but simultaneously keeping an eye on the booth in the corner. Sweaty palms and frizzy hair in my face, I try to quell the knot in my stomach.

Even though I'm not sure what to say and even though I'm worried things with Jesse may never quite go back to how they were, staring at the empty booth in the corner, I realize one thing.

The fear of talking to Jesse, of giving up my family business to be with him, isn't as scary as the prospect of facing a life without him. The empty booth makes me realize that a life without him will be exactly that—empty. The booth, cold and aloof, seems to be illuminated by a spotlight, not just in Midsummer Nights, but in my mind. I can't focus, can't do anything, without noticing the gaping emptiness of it.

Without Jesse, the booth doesn't look right.

Without Jesse, I'm not right, either.

Chapter Twenty-Seven

Jodie, Reed, and Lysander try to convince me to go out for drinks after work. I turn them down. I feel like I need time to think, to figure out what I want to say to Jesse. I head home, take a shower, and grab a sweatshirt. I hook up Henry's leash, needing to get out of the apartment to clear my head. The ocean air, although chilly at this time of year, will do me good.

I put my hood up as Henry and I head toward the boardwalk. It's too cold to go down to the water, so we head for the bench in front of Midsummer Nights. I think about all the times this summer Jesse and I sat on the bench, looking out at the sand and the water. I think about our kisses, our confessions, and our moments there. I think about our late-night walks with Jake and Henry.

I think about how crazy I was to even consider giving it up. Looking at that booth tonight made me feel more empty than the day I found Chris cheating on me. It made me feel worse than the long nights that followed, alone in our bed, thinking about the bleak future.

The breeze chills me, but I welcome its icy fingers grabbing hold of my face. It matches the feel of my heart right now.

"Is this seat taken?" a deep, gritty voice says. My heart chills. I turn to see the green eyes I was just thinking about.

Jake is with him, hooked to a leash. Henry practically pulls me off the bench to see his best friend. I grin, and Jesse pulls Jake toward the bench to sit beside us. After a few moments of being tangled in leashes and interrupted by the joyous barks of two dogs, everyone quiets down. A silence pervades the bench, underscoring the tension between us.

"You didn't come to your booth tonight," I say, not sure how else to start this conversation.

He sighs. "I needed time to just be alone and think about things."

I nod, waiting for him to go on.

"Avery, I know I said I could let you go. I know I said this was what was best. But can I be honest?"

I nod again, still playing the role of a mute.

"I was a fucking moron."

I feel myself jump back a little, surprised at his bluntness. "What do you mean?" I ask, only because it feels like basically the only thing I can say in response.

"I've been miserable since I left the beach that day, since I told you to go. I want you to pursue your dreams. I want you to be happy. But dammit, I don't want to let you go. So if you still want to be with me, if you still love me the way I think you do, then take me with you. Let me come to

Pittsburgh with you."

"What about J & J's?" I ask, stunned by his confession.

"It was my dream when I didn't have anything to cling to in this world. But sometimes dreams change. I have a new dream now, and she's sitting beside me. Dad would want me to be happy. And I can't be that without you. You're my new dream, Avery. I know it's a big risk, and I know love is never promised. But I love you. I'm willing to take the risk."

I look down at my hands, fiddling with a ring I'm wearing. Finally, after I take in everything he's just said, I turn to look at him. "I've been miserable without you, too. I wanted to call you so many times. I wanted to talk to you. But I was scared. I was scared that maybe you letting me go was a sign you weren't feeling what I was. I know that's stupid. But I was insecure and afraid. I'm not taking the job, Jesse. I'm not leaving. My dreams have changed too. I don't want to leave what I've built here. Most of all, I don't want to leave you. I know I promised myself I wouldn't make choices based on love anymore, but you were a game changer. You crossed the line I drew in the sand around my heart. You found your way in. I love you with everything I am. You're worth the risk."

We stare at each other for a long moment, realizing our hearts are true and crystal clear. With Jake and Henry at our feet, we lean into each other, meeting halfway, our lips sealing the words we've just spoken. We kiss to make up for the time we've lost and for the fears we felt of losing each other. We kiss away any doubts we had and our almost goodbye. We kiss ourselves into a new future that still isn't certain, but is steadfast in its own right. We kiss away our previous notions about love.

We kiss, the new versions of Jesse and Avery with new dreams, fewer fears, and more love. When we pull back, we look at each other for a long moment, knowing without a doubt this is right where we both belong.

Our pasts melt away as this new, exciting thing between us promises to be real. We can't wipe away the hurt and rejection we've been through. We can't promise this will be perfect and ideal. We can't promise our love will tattoo itself indelibly on our hearts and outlast every obstacle.

For now, though, we can promise our love is genuine and is what makes us both happy. Our love is what makes me the Avery I've always wanted to be.

So when Jesse looks at me under the starry sky, Henry now snoring at my feet, and asks, "Will you move in with me?" I don't hesitate. I don't think about the rational choice or the safe decision. I don't think about what the old Avery would say or what the Avery from a few months ago would do.

I think in the moment with the clarity of my heart's desire and the feeling in my gut. I turn to Jesse, those green eyes still piercing deep into me, and I say, "I want to jump in with you. All the way in, freezing cold water or not. So, yes."

He kisses me again, and I succumb to the idea that I didn't come here to find love—but it found me anyway.

I realize I'm more than okay with that as our kissing turns more heated and the chilly autumn air warms with the heat from our bodies and the love radiating between us.

Epilogue

A love/hate relationship with parasailing, a confidence in my painting, a new tattoo on my shoulder, a mural painting business, and a taste for fried pickles.

That's some of what he gave me so far... but the list keeps growing every day.

I came here for a new start, a new life, and a pact to not let a man back into this damaged heart of mine. Still, without even planning on it, Jesse found his way into my dented, bruised heart.

Neither of us thought we were ready for this. We told ourselves we weren't ready for love. We thought we were destined to be alone, better off alone.

Once we realized our hearts were inked with a love for each other we couldn't deny, however, we learned sometimes love has different plans than we do. Sometimes you can't fight what wants to be felt. Sometimes you just have to learn to make room for a new plan, a new future, because you realize your life without him isn't really living at all.

I'm not stupid. I've learned the hard way that, like tattoos, love isn't permanent. Even a tattoo can be scorched off with copious amounts of time, money, and pain or changed into something new.

Vows of forever can also be wiped away, obliterated with the monotony of time, the touch of another, or the changing of a heart.

I'm not afraid, though. Jesse's taught me to live free, to dream big, and to go after what I want. I want him with every fiber of my being. When I look at my future, at my dreams, I see him.

We found love in a small tattoo parlor by the sea. Our hearts are inked with our entwined hopes for the future, our infatuation with each other, and our mutual belief we can make a life together.

Love isn't always permanent, and the ink can fade.

Now, though, our hearts are inked on each other, a symbol of our belief in a new start, a new relationship, a new beginning together.

Someday, we might wear our inked hearts on our tattooed sleeves. We might promise ourselves to each other in every way humanly possible. When I look into his eyes, I can see myself standing in the sand, our tattooed wedding rings burning as we say those vows. In his eyes, I see promises for tomorrow, hope for forever, and a burning love I never thought I'd find.

Today, we're okay with wearing our inked hearts on the inside. We're okay with knowing we love each other, with promising to see where that feeling goes. No matter what happens, no matter what tomorrow brings, I know I've found exactly what I was looking for when I came here—myself.

Acknowledgements

Foremost, I want to thank my amazing publisher, Hot Tree Publishing. You have believed in my writing and have helped shape me into the writer I am today. Thank you for always working so hard to help me with my writing and confidence. The family feel at Hot Tree Publishing is something I was looking for but didn't think existed. Thank you for taking me into the family. Thank you to Becky, Claire, Peggy, Olivia, Justine, and everyone else who works so tirelessly to help get my stories into the hands of readers. Thank you to all of the Hot Tree Publishing authors for your constant encouragement and support.

Thank you to my readers. When I started this journey as a small-town girl with a big dream, I didn't know if anyone would ever read my words. You have shown me so much love and support. You've shown me that dreams can come true. Thank you for helping me pursue my wildest dreams.

Thank you to my parents for encouraging me to chase

after my goals, and for showing me the value of working hard. You instilled a love for books and writing within me at a young age. It is because of both of you that I am standing where I am today. Thank you for being tireless fans and supporters.

I want to thank my supportive husband who is always right beside me, on the good days and the bad. On days I felt like giving up on these dreams, you pushed me forward. You are there to encourage me and to remind me of all of the positive things. Whether it's standing for hours in the rain at an outdoor book festival or wearing your shirts around town, you do whatever you can to help my dreams come true. You are my best friend and my soul mate. Thank you for walking this crazy journey called life with me.

Thank you to all of my friends and family who support my writing. A special thanks goes to Christie James, Kelly Rubritz, Carla Firment, Sandra Corey, Lynette Luke, Jennifer Carney, Alycia Schmouder, Kay Shuma, Dr. Letcher, Jamie Lynch, Kristin Books, and Kristin Mathias. Thank you, Grandma Bonnie, for being at every single author event and always supporting my goals. Thank you to my local Barnes & Noble and Bradley's Books for always hosting my author events and graciously welcoming me into your stores.

Thank you to the teachers who shaped my journey, especially Diane Vella, Tom Kunkle, Sue Gunsallus, and all the Mount Aloysius College professors. You gave me the confidence in myself to be a writer and the skills I needed to pursue it.

Last but not least, thank you to my four-legged best

friend, Henry. Even on my worst day, you remind me that there is beauty in every single moment. You're always there to lend a nonjudgmental ear and to eat way too many cupcakes with me. Thank you for all of the memories and for showing me what unconditional love looks like.

About the Author

A high school English teacher, an author, and a fan of anything pink and/or glittery, Lindsay's the English teacher cliché; she loves cats, reading, Shakespeare, and Poe.

She currently lives in her hometown with her husband, Chad (her junior high sweetheart); their cats, Arya, Amelia, Alice, and Bob; and their Mastiff, Henry.

Lindsay's goal with her writing is to show the power of love and the beauty of life while also instilling a true sense of realism in her work. Some reviewers have noted that her books are not the "typical romance." With her novels coming from a place of honesty, Lindsay examines the difficult questions, looks at the tough emotions, and paints the pictures that are sometimes difficult to look at. She wants her fiction to resonate with readers as realistic, poetic, and powerful. Lindsay wants women readers to be able to say, "I see myself in that novel." She wants to speak to the modern woman's experience while also bringing a twist of something new and exciting. Her aim is for readers to say, "That could happen," or "I feel like the characters are real." That's how she knows she's done her job.

Lindsay's hope is that by becoming a published author, she can inspire some of her students and other aspiring writers to pursue their own passions. She wants them to see that any dream can be attained and publishing a novel isn't out of the realm of possibility.

Lindsay loves connecting with readers. She'd love for you to reach out to her.

WEBSITE: WWW.LINDSAYDETWILER.COM
TWITTER: WWW.TWITTER.COM/LINDSAYDETWILER
INSTAGRAM: WWW.INSTAGRAM.COM/LINDSAYANNDETWILER
FACEBOOK: WWW.FACEBOOK.COM/LINDSAYANNDETWILER
NEWSLETTER: HTTP://BIT.LY/2U42BJU

About the Publisher

Hot Tree Publishing opened its doors in 2015 with an aspiration to bring quality fiction to the world of readers. With the initial focus on romance and a wide spread of romance sub-genres, they envision opening up to alternative genres in the near future.

Firmly seated in the industry as a leading editing provider to independent authors and small publishing houses, Hot Tree Publishing is the sister company to Hot Tree Editing, founded in 2012. Having established in-house editing and promotions, plus having a well-respected market presence, Hot Tree Publishing endeavors to be a leader in bringing quality stories to the world of readers.

Interested in discovering more amazing reads brought to you by Hot Tree Publishing or perhaps you're interested in submitting a manuscript and joining the HTPubs family? Either way, head over to the website for information:

WWW.HOTTREEPUBLISHING.COM